10 Women

stories

George Bowering

ANVIL PRESS / VANCOUVER

Anvil Press Publishers Inc.
P.O. Box 3008, Main Post Office
Vancouver, B.C. V6B 3X5 CANADA
www.anvilpress.com

Library and Archives Canada Cataloguing in Publication

Bowering, George, 1935-, author
        10 women / George Bowering. — First edition.

Short stories.
ISBN 978-1-77214-031-6 (paperback)

        I. Title. II. Title: Ten women.

PS8503.O875T45 2015   C813'.54   C2015-905978-X

Printed and bound in Canada
Cover design by Rayola Graphic
Interior by HeimatHouse
Represented in Canada by the Publishers Group Canada
Distributed by Raincoast Books

Canadä

The Canada Council | Le Conseil des Arts
for the Arts | du Canada

BRITISH COLUMBIA
ARTS COUNCIL

The publisher gratefully acknowledges the financial assistance of the Canada Council for the Arts, the Canada Book Fund, and the Province of British Columbia through the B.C. Arts Council and the Book Publishing Tax Credit.

Acknowledgements

Half or more of these stories have been published, perhaps
in slightly different shape, in

The Capilano Review

ti-TCR, a web folio

subTerrain

Rampike

West Coast Line

Thanks to the BC Arts Council for support on this project.
"Ichiko" comes from an idea from Jean Baird.

DEDICATION

or homage to Michael Rumaker, Gilbert Sorrentino,
and Fielding Dawson

CONTENTS

Melody

Most of the time I don't look at the obituary pages, because I know I'll look at the birth dates and get all upset because so many of them are later than my own. You ever notice that? But sometimes lately I have looked at them, hoping like hell I won't see anyone I know, and maybe secretly a little thrilled at the prospect.

Prospect—is that right?

Sometimes I do see someone I know, or someone that the people I know know better than I do. I usually gain a little more knowledge about that person's life than I formerly had. One day last spring, I remember it was spring because when I picked up the newspaper I saw the first daffodils near our front porch, I found out that a sculptor I kind of knew had a PhD in economics. I had always thought he was a kind of street kid who stuck to his art and made it in a medium way.

Daffodils were called asphodels in the olden days. I suppose someone knows how and when the letter dee got up there in front. Asphodels and daffodils have been used in poetry since who remembers when. I wandered lonely as a cloud. Asphodel, the greeny flower, said some other poet. You know that daffodils are in the amaryllis family, another member of which is supposed to have sprung up around the pool where Narcissus drowned after staring at himself too long. That's poetry. It seems as if all those ancient Greek flowers were related to one another.

Anyway, the main thing about asphodels is that they grew like crazy all over the Elysian Fields, where dead people had to live after crossing over into Hades. So you see.

Anyway, it's late fall now, and what I see when I open the front door and bend over to pick up the newspaper is a lot of brown maple leaves. When I do this I usually think well, that didn't take long!

So one morning I came in and sat at the dining room table with my first cup of coffee and the newspaper. First, as always, I did the *New York Times* crossword. It was Wednesday, so it wasn't all that hard. With my ink pen I told it that the hero of the Polo Grounds was Ott, meaning Mel Ott, who, when I was a kid, held the National League record for lifetime home runs. 511. Cy Young had the record for wins as a pitcher. 511. Looks like an important phone number.

Then I read the sports pages, which in late fall are pretty boring. Baseball had been over for a month, and hockey and football were all over the place. Basketball is just not as interesting as it used to be when it was about teams. Then I read the first section and the second section and so on, and finished up with the white comics. This day, as often happens, they were across from the obituary page. On Wednesday there was usually only one obituary page.

The usual stuff, bad poetry, which is all right because it is kind of sweet that human beings will try poetry at such a time, don't you think? I checked the dates, I read some of the bad poems, and I gave a moment or two to the survived-bys. And I had a look at the photographs. You're seeing more and more photographs on the obit pages nowadays. Sometimes the survived-bys will put in two photographs, one from when the person was young, and another one from recent times.

But the photograph that started all my trouble was a recent amateur headshot of someone named Melody Danton. Under the picture was a little verse: "Death is a hurt no one can heal, / love is a memory no one can steal." Then a simple list: "Your loving husband Roger, Mom, Dad, and family." Just above these words I read: "In loving memory of Melody Danton / July 25, 1962–Sept 12, 2010."

She had died two years ago. But I could not put the paper away. I looked and looked at her face. How, I asked I don't know whom, can this woman not be alive?

It was not the first time I had noticed how alive the people looked on the obituary pages, but then I usually fold the paper and put it with the week's other papers, and head upstairs to work, or at least look at my email. On this occasion, and what a stupid phrase that is, I looked and looked.

I am not good at describing people's appearances. I always

give up rather than mention eye colour or hair style. When someone asks hey, did you get a load of that woman in the red dress at the Stevens's party, I always have to confess that I don't remember what colours anyone was wearing. I am not very good at colours anyway, but I don't know—I can never figure out what use it is to try to describe someone. Maybe if he walks around with a hatchet buried in his skull, okay, I will mention that.

So I will not try to tell you everything I saw in the little black and white amateur photograph of Melody Danton. But while I was sitting with my elbows on the dining room table and my chin on my fists under my cheekbones, I looked at an open friendly face that seemed more and more as if Melody Danton were looking back at me.

And as if she were just beginning to smile.

Every once in a while something happens, you notice something, something that you know right then is not just ordinary business. These things usually happen while you are doing something you do every day. A name is said on the radio. There is a package just outside the front door. Okay, I thought, tomorrow I will just remember this obit as a particularly effective one. I won't mention it to anyone on email. I won't remember her name after an hour or so at my desk.

But you know that didn't work. Otherwise I wouldn't be telling you all this. I thought about that face all the rest of the day. I cut the obit notice out of the paper and taped it to the upper right corner of my computer. I wasted a few hours in total, I guess, just looking at it, my chin in my hand. I looked at it again the next day, and I read that poor little couplet over and over, long after I knew it by heart. I was spending more time looking at a tiny picture of Melody Danton than I was on my email and the short story I was supposed to be writing.

If only I could have met Melody Danton. She might have had a coarse sense of humour, or she might have liked reading books about vampires. Then I would have been able to stay away, or forget her altogether. She might have watched hit television shows or worn a New York Yankees baseball cap. But all I had was that little picture of a face that seemed to be sending vectors of fondness right at me.

On the fourth day I decided to find out more about her, if only to learn something that would set me free from her gaze. Was she fond of Las Vegas, maybe? Did she say "begs the question" when she meant "raises the question"? What if I found out that she was totally loving and totally lovable, and I had missed her whole life, the forty-eight years that other people had enjoyed? All those thousands of tiny moments. I can see her with a bowl and a wooden spoon, having just spooned the cake mix into the pan, that lovely look on her fair face.

Where to start? I wished that Roger and her parents had been as detailed as some of the notices you see. "Patricia attended Lord Byng High School and u.b.c., then took a position with West Coast Cedar Homes," etc., etc. But these were new deaths, of course. Melody's was one of those annual notices purchased to show that the family hasn't forgotten. All I had to do was have a look through the paper of two years ago.

But what could I do without going there? First I looked around the Internet, to see whether she had ever done anything to make her the slightest bit famous. The only real hit I got on my search engine was a blog for people involved with TED, an organization for individuals who wanted to spread their ideas at conferences. It was something I might want to look into later, but right now I was in search of a real woman. Well, a woman who had passed away without my noticing two years ago.

So what about the phone book? In the last few years the phone book had become three or four different kinds of phone book, with white pages, yellow pages, blue pages and lord knows what else. It was getting so that I couldn't figure out how to look up a person's telephone number. But I gave it a try. In our kitchen, I found out, there are four thick telephone books, and guess what? They are all for business names. Some of them have yellow pages and white pages, but they're just two ways of looking up a business. If you are a person instead of a business, I can't phone you from my place.

Unless I get onto the computer. Ah, Christ! Okay, if you type "telephone numbers" into the appropriate box on the screen, the machine will find you a page that features black fingers walking in a yellow space—just like the phone book. From there it doesn't take too long for you to persuade the machine that you do not want to look up a business. You can find telephone numbers for those people who have somehow listed them. I typed in "Danton," and the name of the province, and up came four numbers for the whole shebang. After that the D'Antonios start.

One of the Dantons lived way up in 100 Mile House. One was in Vancouver, and the other two were in Surrey. The one up north had one of those first names that could designate either sex. The three others all went by initials, and one of the initials was M! Okay, I thought, it could be that no one changed the name on the phone number after Melody passed away. It could be that these were men's phone numbers, though it is my experience that when you see initials before a phone number, they are there to ward off those cretins that call up women and talk dirty to them.

I decided to go to all the hassle of looking up the original obit notice. The Internet is good for something once in a while, and almost makes up for its many crimes on one of those occasions when you do use it. It took a while, but I learned how to use my bedimmed wits to "access," as they say, the paper's back files. I knew that she had died on September 12, so I checked out the paper for September 13, but just found a dozen other newly dead. On September 14, there she was—the same photo. I stared at her face for maybe ten minutes before reading the words underneath. As it turned out, I didn't learn much more than when I started. About all I got that I hadn't had were the names of her parents—Thomas and Louise Cater. I was hoping that I would have found out her place of birth at least, but no such luck. And I guessed that "family" in the later notice did not include any children. Roger and Melody were apparently without issue.

Just to see whether it would be of any use, I looked up the name Cater at canada411.ca. I was very speedily informed that there was no such name listed in British Columbia, but that there were Caters galore in the province of Quebec. Two pieces of information that discouraged me. I was unlikely ever to find Melody via her probably French-Canadian family. I would have to see what success I might find through the Dantons.

Of course, the Dantons were probably French Canadian. Quebec was probably full of Dantons.

I would have to phone my four Dantons. Unfortunately, I am a telephone-shy person. I would wait a day, to try to think what to say to these people. In the meantime I took a good long look at that little black-and-white picture.

It took me a week to get up the nerve to phone any of the Dantons I had found numbers for. What a relief I felt when the first one I tried, the one in Burnaby, didn't answer the phone. I didn't even wait for the invitation to leave a message. I'd try another one tomorrow, I decided. Whew, I added.

Actually, I waited for two days and then tried phoning the Danton in Surrey, at a cellphone number. I tried it twice, and both times got an automated but full-throated female voice telling me that the number I had dialed had been discontinued, or withdrawn or cancelled, or some such verb. I thought that I had better try it again to make the verb clear. But this time an older female voice answered, and I don't know whether she was speaking French or English or some other language. Had I dialed the wrong number this time? Or the previous time? Unfortunately, I had already drawn a line of ink across the number, and could not be sure whether I was looking at a five or a three.

I just said, "Sorry, I think I have a wrong number."

"No problem," the voice said in a kind way, and in English.

Now what? I could either contact canada411.ca to get a clean printout of the numbers, or I could ask my wife to have a look at the number I had crossed out.

In any case, I decided to wait till tomorrow, so the woman, whether a Danton or not, would not be worried. Phew again.

But in the later afternoon—well, just a block away, on the corner of 10ᵗʰ Avenue, there's a handy print shop, where I sometimes go to get silly little jobs done. So I took the obit, picture, and words to the print shop to have it, what do you call it when you get a card or something encased in plastic? First I had trimmed it a bit more with my desk scissors. Took them about five minutes, and now I had a little black-and-white newspaper picture of Melody Danton to carry around with me. Even on the way home from the store I took it out of my shirt pocket just to check that they had got it right. I stopped walking for a good minute and a half and looked at that wonderful face. She didn't look any the less alive for being inside airtight plastic.

Then in the morning, or rather about noon, after all my delaying tactics—I read every section of the Thursday paper, read all my email and answered some of it, and then answered some older messages, threw some really old tax records into the yellow bag, ran the day's envelopes through the shredder—I took a breath and called the other Surrey number, also a cellphone.

"Hello," said a pleasant old guy's voice, throat being cleared at the same time.

"I'm probably on a wild goose chase," I said. "I'm looking for someone named Melody Danton."

"You say Melody?" It was hard to tell whether it was going to be a yes or a no, probably a no. "No one named Melody in our family."

"Ah, I figure I'm on a wild goose chase," I said. This wasn't so bad once I'd got started. "She died about two years ago. I used to know her back in Montreal in the early seventies."

"Nope. No Melody in our family. But you know, what was that, about 1970? That's about when our family came out from Montreal . . ."

"Yes, 1970, 1971."

"So how old was she when she died?"

"Oh, well, late fifties, I guess."

"Quite a few Dantons in Montreal, I guess," the nice old guy said. He had a kind of friendly working-class voice, the kind you find in smaller towns all over the country.

"Well, thanks," I said. "I didn't think—but I figured I'd give it a try. Thanks."

It wasn't all that much of a relief when we hung up. Not that I would ever be able to do a job in which you had to call people up on the telephone. As bad as the job I had for one day when I was a kid, going from door to door trying to sell tomatoes. I wound up giving them away for a dollar, and didn't have that job any more.

Laminated, that's it.

On Friday I didn't have to make one of the phone calls, because I got an email requesting that I revise a little bit of prose I had written to accompany a poem that was going to be in an anthology of poems about other poets. It took me a while to do it, but only because I could not figure out how to work on the files they sent me and had to start all over on the little bit of prose. But I considered that to be writing work, a day properly lived, so I didn't have to make a phone call to a Danton and report it here.

On Saturday I fiddled and dawdled, and eventually put in a long-distance call to the Cariboo. I got a British woman's voice on the answering machine, and left a little message about phoning later to ask about Melody. That got me off free for another day. I thought about writing a fictional phone call, but rules are rules, even if you make them up yourself, especially if you make them up yourself, maybe.

In any case, I worked up the nerve to call again on Sunday, and after five or six rings, just when I was getting ready to hang up, the same woman, I think, answered. I introduced myself, and she handed me over to her husband. I introduced myself again, and when we began talking I knew that the northern Dantons had discussed the question of a Melody Danton in the interim. We had a pretty good breezy discussion, in which I learned that the British name Danton had once been French, having arrived in southeast England during and after the invasion of 1066. I told him about Quebec and the Dantons there, and we smilingly offered our apologies, mine for bothering him, his for not being able to help.

"She would have been your girlfriend, then?" he asked.

"In a manner of speaking," I said.

Next day another little writing job came in on the Internoise, and I was able to put phoning off for another day. But the day after that, after I had done all my tidying, all my easy email, the thing I sometimes do with my especially bad toenail, I worked up the nerve to make another call. I had two numbers left, and one of them was out of commission. I decided to give it one more chance. There was no sweat on my eyelids, but my pulse rate and my blood pressure were both up, even though I was expecting an automatic announcement of failure. But somewhere a phone rang six times, and then a recorded voice told me about its owner's regret that she could not be there to talk with me. She then said some lovely things about my well-being, and performed an unlikely combination of wistfulness and perkiness in her goodbye.

When I pushed the red END button on my phone, I was short of breath. I vowed then to give this telephoning business more thought.

On the one hand, I had been reading *Pig Earth* by John Berger. In an introductory chapter he wrote, " . . . the writing becomes, as soon as I begin, a struggle to give meaning to experience." That's on page six.

Well, I had to agree with him about struggle, and I was at least open to the idea, or maybe hope, of meaning—maybe not giving it, but possibly finding it. That's not the main reason that people make telephone calls these days, but if you are nervous the way I am, you need some kind of push.

I do remember something that Chris Danton in the Cariboo had told me. He said that in recent times there have been quite a few Dantons showing up in the Vancouver area. I hadn't thought about it at the time, but now I've come to wonder whether he'd been talking about his kids migrating from the north down to the Coast.

So you see where I am heading? If he doesn't know anything about a Melody Danton, it's a pretty sure bet that his kids won't either.

That was just what I needed. I wouldn't have to get up the moxie to make any more phone calls to people I don't know. The anxiety was not worth it, and in fact I could feel it slipping sideways off my shoulders.

And really, what is so special about falling in love, if that's what this was, with a woman you will never be able to meet? Haven't you ever seen a woman sitting at another table or shouldering her snow-touched fur coat through a revolving door, and felt a sudden sense of loss because other people get to talk with her and share memories with her and you don't, and you know that this could happen if you were in, I don't know, Zagreb instead of here? I look at pictures of my wife when she was a college girl with a long single braid and a tanned face, and I yearn for her.

Still, I see all those photographs on the obituary pages, and yes, I do see so much life in the faces there, but then I can turn the page. I can't do that with Melody Danton, not by a long shot. I know almost nothing about her. I will never find Roger Danton, not that I would ever want to. I don't know the first thing about him and I am jealous of his many days. I have that little amateur picture encased in plastic, whatever you call it, and no, I am not in love with a dead woman, not in love. It's just—that look on that sweet face. It's awful to have, but you can't just toss it away, can you?

Stephanie

I have been advised that before I tell you what Stephanie did to me and maybe why she did it, I should tell you about her, describe her, I guess.

Well, I wonder whether you remember that girl from your high school class, the one with the height. I mean she's as tall as you or just about, or at least it seems as if she is, and everything she has is long. She has long arms, sort of thin but still the kind you imagine sniffing and kissing and maybe later having around you, or maybe even earlier. And similarly her legs, they are long and a bit thin, or at least from the knees up they seem to be almost as narrow as they are from the knees down. You know what I mean, eh?

Just a little bit of light, light, downy hair on the backs of her arms, such as you might not notice unless the sunlight was just right. Skin takes on a beautiful light tan in the summer, totally even, not a freckle in sight, not a scar, no marks at all, just a hardly discernible drift of faint hairs on that skin, which I know you could not feel with your sensitive fingers.

I have to admit that I have always liked long narrow arms on a woman, starting with on a girl and going on till there's probably flesh hanging off her triceps. I have noticed in nice weather that women blessed with those long thin arms with a bit of tan to them seem to like to wear white sleeveless shirts or blouses or tops or whatever they are calling them at the time.

"What are you looking at?"

This is a girl with long thin bare arms in science class, ninth grade. I sort of knew later that she'd enjoyed having them looked at, but I was pretty dumb about such things in grade nine. I knew the valence of zinc and the principle of photosynthesis, but I didn't know much about the way girls' minds worked. I made the mistake of thinking that they were just like boys' minds. I am puzzled by things like that. In the last day or two I have talked with two women who have never been bothered by the fact that they don't know which way is north. I'd go nuts not knowing. Or people who see French writing on packages and aren't curious to know what it's saying. I can't imagine looking at words and not trying to read them.

I think that Stephanie knew which way was north, pretty sure she knew what *blé entier* is. That's not important here— we are focusing on her arms, her arms and her legs. But now I'm thinking: I wonder why I started with her arms when it came to describing her. I get the idea that before I tell you what she did to me and why she did it, I ought to describe the woman. But no one ever told me to start with arms. I don't imagine that very many people in a similar situation would start with arms. Probably most people would start with the face and hair, maybe. A guy that's a tit man, as they say, might start there, but how often that happens I couldn't say. Or if a woman has gigantic ears, maybe there would be a reason to start with her ears—but then there might as easily be a reason to end there, after a kind of climactic buildup through the rest of her features.

Or, yes, what about hair? If I had been trying to capture the beauty of Stephanie's hair in, say, 1885, I might have proceeded this way: her face had the usual fullness of expression which is developed by a life of solitude. Where the eyes of a multitude continuously beat like waves upon a countenance they seem to wear away its mobile power; but in the still water of privacy every feeling and sentiment unfolds in visible luxuriance, to be interpreted as readily as a printed word by an intruder. In years she was no more than nineteen or twenty, but the necessity of taking thought at a too early period of life had forced the provisional curves of her childhood's face to a premature finality. Thus she had but little pretension to beauty, save in one prominent particular—her hair.

Okay, I actually started with her height before I got to the long narrow arms. Or at least the idea of height, not *her* height particularly, but women and girls of a certain height. When I see a short guy with a tall woman I often think what a lucky son of a gun. Well, you can just imagine. Stephanie, as I said, was just about as tall as I was, and I had to stand on tiptoe to kiss her forehead. But as well as long arms, tall girls usually have big feet, and I have never seen anything particularly good about big feet. I suppose that there are men who salivate over big feet on a woman, I mean speaking as a figure of speech. My buddy Willy was always in favour of muscular legs on a girl, and I myself have always taken an odd pleasure in looking at slightly too thick ankles. But big feet?

Especially in those slip-on shoes. No, sir.

Okay, Stephanie's feet were big, or let's say long, maybe long and narrow, or rather narrow for their length. Her hands were kind of big too, which I didn't mind at all. She had long, long fingers, and I still imagine them holding me by my bare waist. She could also easily wrap them around my neck, which she did more than once. Sometimes I would put my palm against hers and see that her fingers were a little longer than mine. Once she tickled my palm with her long narrow forefinger, or rather its pointy fingernail, and I came really close to you know what in my shorts.

Long nose, I guess. Long thighs. Long back. Beautiful suntanned naked long back. I used to enjoy kissing her vertebrae, or rather the skin over her vertebrae, didn't matter which direction, one by one. Long tongue. Nice long neck.

I can only imagine those things now, after what has happened. I want to get to that, but from what I have heard, the story won't make any sense unless I describe Stephanie for you. If you could only see her the way I first saw her. It was my first day at the creek, you know, where it slides out lazily after passing under the Union Street bridge? There's a picnic table there on a bit of lawn above the creek. I had been thinking for some time of taking my lunch down there and eating my egg sandwich in the October sunshine. It was that same sunshine that made it hard to see Stephanie that first time.

She was pushing her bicycle toward where I was sitting, just unwrapping the cling stuff from my tomato sandwich. The sun was behind her and so low that I couldn't even tell at first whether it was a man or a woman pushing the bicycle. She was so tall, you understand. But when she got to where I was sitting, and leaned her bicycle against one end of the picnic table, I saw that hair. It was mixed with sunshine when she pulled off her helmet and shook her head, sunshine and silk looking the way you wished the creek would look instead of just sliding along flat.

She was wearing the tightest blue jeans I had ever seen up till then. If she had had anything on under those jeans, I would have seen a line made by elastic or cotton. When she sat, she sat on top of the piano, next to my sandwich. I was eye level to her chest, and thankful for the warm October weather. All she had over her breasts was a confused bit of cloth, I don't know, some kind of rayon, maybe. I was not thinking clearly, and I thought that my eyes were in trouble.

I remembered pretty well exactly what my creative writing class on description said:

Tips on how to use description as a tool to add depth and texture to a piece of creative writing.

Description is a useful tool for bringing a story to life but should not be overdone. Here are some useful tips that can improve anybody's creative writing.

Ditch the Mundane.

Don't use bland descriptions such as the dog was brown or her hair was dark blonde. Introduce depth and texture by saying the Labrador was the shade of melted chocolate or her hair was the colour of caramel fudge.

I don't know. I have never wanted to eat a dog or even Stephanie's hair. But these creative writing teachers know what they are talking about. A lot of them have published stories or even books.

So all right. Stephanie's hair was the colour of caramel fudge. It was also the colour of caramel toffee and caramel ice cream. When she put the fingers of both hands in it and sprayed them apart, her hair seemed to fling light from itself, a kind of caramel light. Or more like butterscotch light. Or are they the same thing? That's one of those things I have always wondered. Like groin and crotch. Are they the same thing? When I was reading sports magazines as a kid I would find out that Kyle Rote or Hal Newhouser or someone had a groin injury, a pulled groin or something, and I didn't know where the groin is. I figured it must be that connection between your shoulder and your neck. Mine was often sore, and in fact it's sore right now.

I just looked back and saw that I have her sitting on the piano. I must have meant the picnic table, because that's where I was at the time. I could easily go back and change that, but I kind of like the piano idea. It was a gleaming black baby grand piano, rubbed at the corners so that a kind of warm brown showed through. The brown of a dog. I was sitting on the piano bench, my short fingers spread out on the keys. She was sitting on the piano, her long naked legs crossed, her diaphanous skirt hiked so high that my heart skipped a beat, and so did my short fingers, turning the tune, "They Call It Stormy Monday" it was, into a kind of rebop exercise.

She laughed that husky way she had of laughing, which was always a surprise, because her speaking voice was gentle and pretty high pitched. I guess she sounded a little like Marilyn Monroe, but without the determined ditzy colouring. So now she laughed without constraint or exaggeration at my awkwardness on the keys. I could have stopped and dramatically put the cover down, but I played instead, my heart beating as if it could get out of its cage. I played another lovely standard, I don't recall which, but I will bet that it was "Just the Way You Look Tonight." I had Helen Forrest in my mind's ear, but Stephanie's long naked legs in my body's eyes. I have hardly ever in my life wanted to do something more than I wanted to put my hand on a long whitish thigh right then. But you know me—I did no such thing.

I didn't know how to stop this, but she took hold of the situation, bouncing down off the piano and pushing her bicycle up the grass slope to Union Street. Those were the tightest jeans I had ever seen up till then, which was the mid-eighties, if you think that is relevant. I know, I know, relevant to what, *m'sieur*.

Those jeans were tight as the tissue wrapped around a human heart. That sounds good. And we don't ask whether it is right, because it is a simile, which we make in order to "cut through logic into the core of the experience." Her stretch-denim-clad legs were as long as the distance between your heart and your heart's aim. Maybe that's a conceit. I have never been able exactly to figure out what a conceit is. I think it is a kind of push-the-limit simile. Well, I am not supposed to be talking or rather writing about what I am writing, but rather preparing you to understand what it meant when Stephanie did what she did to me.

She was so far away from me now as I put all my lunch garbage together, but I can tell you—her eyes were as green as the floor of the forest east of Masset on the north shore of Haida Gwaii. People always come back from Haida Gwaii and tell you what a magical place it is, and never give you any real description of the place. The fog is spectral, the moss is magical, and so on. Her breasts moving loosely inside whatever that silky stuff was were like the promises your parents always made when they were urging you not to grow up so fast.

I'm no fool. I know that similies are like any other lies—fun to believe but suspect. I also know that anybody's description of anyone or anything is just like that, just one angle. So I decided to ask other people how they would describe Stephanie.

"Generous. A very generous person in her own special way," said her friend April. She looked thoughtful while she was saying it.

"I'd say voluptuous is not too strong a word," said Polly Simpson, a woman who had just come to town a year ago but had made friends with Stephanie in no time. "Yes, I have never said that about anyone before, but I have to say Stephanie is voluptuous. In a good way."

"The first word I would come up with would be haughty," said Dana Simpson, Polly's little sister. "Something like haughty."

"Cold and unapproachable." Those are the words of Stephanie's kid brother David. David is twelve years younger than his sister. He was, we all figured, one of those accidents, a kid born long after the family seemed complete.

"Very courteous. Well-spoken. I'd say polite and caring." So said Michael Venables, her film studies professor at Langara College.

"Kind of disturbing," offered Marlene Simpson, Polly and Dana's mother. "I always felt a little creeped when she was over here with the girls."

I asked about ten other people, and I always got the same thing—abstract words. Sometimes contradictory ones, as you can see, but always abstract. I don't know why it is that when you ask anyone to describe someone, they always come up with abstract words. Amazing. Tolerant. Awesome. Beautiful. Thoughtful. If the person you were asking about had a 44-inch bosom, they would say friendly or cheerful or stingy.

So abstract words don't seem to do the trick: the trick being to describe someone to someone else. And similies don't really do it, either. So what will? I go back to those simple things. Stephanie has long thin arms. Her teeth are closer to white than to yellow. Her hair is usually a half-tamed brownish blondish pile on her head and shoulders. Her chest moves around when she walks in high heels, shoes I believe to be a terrible torture for women but which push a woman's thighs forward and make her chest waggle. In theory I am against them.

But I saw Stephanie barefoot more often than I saw her in high heels. And thank goodness, because when she was barefoot she was a tad shorter than I am. Not that this mattered, considering what she did to me. Last winter her feet were tanned until late February. My own feet were tanned till late December in a pattern that resembled my favourite Merrell sandals.

Actually, with all that stuff about the table that was a piano for a while, Stephanie sitting on it with long legs and later walking away—with all that stuff I was slipping into, I don't know, narrative, too soon, because I am supposed to be establishing something by describing my central character. Okay, in real life she is just Stephanie, the woman I love, or rather loved, I should say. When I come to telling you about her, she gets to be a central character. According to the creative writing teachers, you give your central character a lot more description than you give the other characters. She's a round character, someone said, as opposed to flat characters. Like 3D, I suppose.

Central. If you stop and think about it, that seems like a funny word, central. Like everything that happens happens on all sides of her. Now, if the purpose of describing her is to prepare us for understanding what she did, does it make sense saying what she did to stuff and about stuff on all sides

of her? Do you see what I am getting at? Or does it matter?
I could just jump ahead. See that? Ahead—not in all direc-
tions. I could just jump ahead and tell you what she said
when she picked up the telephone and called that auction-
eer. Maybe I should just sort of hint at things like that while
I am trying to fix Stephanie in your imagination.

Oh, *there's* a phrase. Fix Stephanie. We will verb that
noun. Okay, I'm sorry.

We both used to sweat like horses when we made love. I
could feel the sweat in my hair and in the small of my back,
but it was Stephanie's sweat that I loved. By the time we
got it going she was shining all over. I would say glistening
but that sounds like a word you'd expect too easily. I looked
up at her face and the roots of her hair, that glow I wanted
to consume. I saw the light on her perfect breasts and knew
that nowhere in the world would I ever see anything so
lovely. I have seen the sun rise on Bora Bora. I have looked
at light coming through the Hope Diamond. I have seen the
grace of Donatello's hand in the wood of his *Magdalena*.
Wonderful. The sweat on Stephanie's breasts, or should I
say Stephanie's breasts with her sweat on them, in the light
that came on a December morning through our bedroom
window.

And then to look and see the sweat on her thigh, to feel the
sweat drip from her breast to land on mine. I may be trying
to describe this person to make her a character, but I can't describe Stephanie sitting on me, covered with her sweat and
maybe some of mine.

I love that shine. I can't help it. I loved it when Stephanie came home from her run along the beach and up our street. She'd come in breathing hard and glimmering. I had to follow her into the bathroom, and I didn't care whether I got asked into the shower with her, as long as I got to see that sweat on her skin. She'd be all wet coming out of the shower, too, of course, and while that was pretty nice, as you might imagine, it was a far cry from Stephanie and her sweat.

Afterward, in the king-size bed Stephanie would lie on her back, her arms flung out and her feet far apart, and I would get an erection again just looking at her. The bed would be shining too. It was made of beautiful brown wood with wide panels at the head and foot. These I would polish just about every day. I kept my chamois and the tub of furniture wax in the ensuite, and most days after I had brushed my teeth and combed my hair I would take rag and wax and chamois to the lovely cool wood for a while.

You know when that bed looked really lovely? When it was dark outside the window and there were four or five candles burning in the bedroom, and this was terrific even before Stephanie came up to bed—even if she didn't, as a matter of fact. The soft light that came off the wood could not have been created if it were not for the deliciousness of the wood. If I was alone and naked in that candlelight I wouldn't really have an erection, but I would feel a stirring, that's for sure.

It wasn't just the bed, either. I used lemon stuff from a spray can on the dining room table, next to the bed maybe my favourite piece of furniture. It was black in places, brown in other places, carved shapes in the top, not images but patterns, something Japanese, or maybe Korean.

I made love with Stephanie on top of that table just once. She was gorgeous in her sweat and I dined on her with the scent of lemons all over. But after she went up to her room to work, I got out the cloth and wiped that table dry and then I polished it till you could have seen it shining from across the street.

And there was the neat old Oriental chest of drawers. Oh, we kept an odd assortment of things in those many little drawers. It stood about as tall as Stephanie or me, and it had two sets of little drawers, about ten on each side. Batteries, candles, scotch tape, business cards, a couple of Oriental fans. I'll bet I wouldn't be able to remember all the things we kept there if you gave me all afternoon. But stuff in a little drawer can accumulate dust and grime and so on. So just about every day I would empty one or two of the little drawers and wipe the scissors clean if that's what was in there, make sure all the candles were facing the same way.

Then I'd get a soft rag I used to use for cleaning my eyeglasses, and get at the wood on the inside of those little drawers. Do the corners with a Q-tip. Then a bit of spray polishing. I always felt good when I had refilled the drawer and shoved it into place. Every few days I would polish the exterior wood. The chest of drawers stood in the corner of the dining room, with a rich shiny wooden Buddha on a piece of lace on top of it. The glow off the nice old Oriental wood—if this chest of drawers had been a person I would have kissed it then. Well, I did once or twice.

So I miss those things. Where has it gone, the visionary gleam? Didn't someone say that? I am not claiming that a nice clean polished table or whatever is an act of poetry. The question is: what about that act of Stephanie's? Was that poetry? I think it might have been, at least according to her. Poetic justice, maybe? I'm getting silly here. But listen: if what she did to me is poetry, I will stick with prose. As soon as I can do it, I am going to tell the real story, but as I was taught, I have to start by giving you Stephanie as a central character. As soon as I can get calmed down a little, I will describe that beautiful rancorous woman.

Dodie

As far as I know, the business with the unfortunate animals started with the lyrics of a rough and ready poet by the name of Jack Verge. Verge started off in the second wave of mimeograph poets of the late sixties and early seventies. He had come down to Toronto from the scrabbly forest country around Timmins, driving a greasy and very noisy pickup truck, and carrying a thousand sheets of paper with sentimental violence typed all over them.

Let me give you an idea of what I am referring to. Here's a short passage from an early poem called "I Tried Not to Weep":

I put the barrel of the .303 back of the mare's eye
and hesitated, she was looking at me without rancor.
"Shoot the worthless piece of crap," said the boss's son
and I did not point the muzzle at him . . .

The mare did not point hers, either, I thought at the time. I don't think that kind of wordplay was noticed much by the poet. He didn't play much in those days. Ten years later a poem presumably about a bear began:

> When I sliced her open a slick foetus
> was impaled on my knife. Hello, Teddy,
> I said, around my home-made cigarette

And so it went, as Jack Verge made his way into anthologies, and eventually had books published by small presses in Ontario and New Brunswick. With his fourth book, *Blood and Fur,* he made it onto the shortlist for the Alexander Mac-Gregor Rose Prize.

The Canada Council started supporting public readings at colleges and art galleries, and Jack Verge joined such figures as Milton Acorn, Joe Rosenblatt and John Robert Colombo on stages around the province and eventually across the country. Hundreds of poetic animals and birds were maimed and killed, and soon human beings joined them: women clobbered by their men in trailer camps, men meeting their mortality in barroom brawls and mining accidents.

One night in downtown Toronto, at a reading sponsored by the new League of Canadian Poets, Jack Verge gave a reading with a tough new woman poet named Martina Strood. Strood wrote short poems in which people's gardens and public parks were disfigured. At this reading, which took place in the back room of a semi-popular bar on Queen Street, the audience, which numbered three dozen casually dressed listeners, included three obstreperous poets from an entirely different aesthetic. Rather than remaining silent until it came time to applaud politely, these wags kept up what one of them later described as "The Jack Verge Death Count."

Jack read his poem about the bantam rooster that got kicked to death.

"One!" shouted the trio of troublemakers.

Jack lit a cigarette and read his short poem about the hamster in the garburator.

"Two!" they shouted in perfect unison.

And so it went. Jack started reading louder, and it appeared as if he were actually selecting his most gruesome or violent poems to read. The final count for the evening was twenty-four. It might have gone higher if it weren't a joint reading. The hecklers did not respond to the mayhem done to plants by Ms. Strood.

The Jack Verge Death Count happened a few more times, but it did not deter the phenomenon this story is about.

As Jack became better known, and even before he got his first "trade" book publication by what Toronto lit-people call a "major professional publisher," suffering animals starting showing up all over the poetry map. Nobody paid any attention to the few poems that might have, if one looked at them in a certain way, suggested suicidal thoughts. Acolytes of the author of *Bone Bruises* peppered the journals with fauna abuse. Michael Ondaatje published "Rat Jelly." Pat Lane chimed in with a dog who can't puke up the bones of a bird he has swallowed. "Go now/ you who would weep at his dying," we were advised poetically. Even Martina Strood branched out, offering poems about drowned turkeys and layered roadkill. When the 1973 Alexander McGregor Rose Prize shortlist came out, three of the five finalists had the word "Blood" in their titles.

But it didn't stop with the poets. In 1974 the Major-General's award for fiction went to a novel titled *Bare*, about a woman who disrobes in the forest and frightens all the animals to death.

Okay, that part was made up. But there was a big rise in the number of novels and short stories from coast to coast about the mistreatment of our animal life, both wild and domestic. The playwrights were soon to follow. It will be a long time before Halifax playgoers forget the single performance of *Quills*, Seamus MacDonald's play in which a porcupine is clubbed to death by three women wielding seal-hunter clubs. MacDonald got the resulting street protest and subsequent riot down on 16-millimetre colour film.

Then there was a tidal wave of confessional autobiographies and other non-fiction works, detailing the shocking and cruel behaviour of well-known writers, politicians, sports figures and entertainers. I know at least four people who threw up or otherwise reacted organically to the infamous pelican scene in the memoir of a very highly regarded Greco-Canadian literary critic.

Pretty soon the Canadian pop-music world was inundated with faunacide. A hit-parade chart from the summer of 1974 will provide these titles: for example, "Skinning Fluffy," "I Ate a Penguin Last Night," "Hanging from My Leash," and the top hit of that season, "Airedale Jam."

Around this time, Jack Verge was riding high on the stages of all the independent art galleries in the country, except the ones ruled by those louts who started the Jack Verge Death Count. Posters for his readings always showed him leaning on his crumpled pickup truck, or holding a shotgun under his arm. His young fans showed up in plaid shirts and laced boots, grasping worn sheets of typing paper, hoping for an open mike. His readings would often be accompanied by unusual action art, often including snakes and other unhappy reptiles. The person he called his "woman" seldom showed up. She was encumbered with ill-dressed children.

I interviewed him one time for a weekly paper you could pick up free in any of the less fancy restaurants and cafes in Toronto.

"What's with all these brutalized animals and women?" I asked.

"Read Neruda. It's all in there," he said.

Most people will remember the story of Sniffy, the brown and white rat who made it into all the newspapers for a few weeks in the fall of 1974. Inspired by stories that some art students in Quebec had guillotined a sheep during a "happening," Vancouver artist Rick Gibson built a box for his Sniffy the art project. The box had a Plexiglas wall through which art patrons could watch the action, a floor made of painter's canvas, and a ceiling hole through which Gibson could drop a 25-kilogram concrete block. The newspapers and local television stations played along as they can be expected to do with this kind of stunt, and pretty soon big crowds appeared at the Vancouver Art Gallery steps for the rehearsals.

Gibson, who a year earlier had claimed to be eating a friend's severed testicle at the same site, set the date for Sniffy's execution, and the middle class went berserk. Several times he had to run for his life, carrying Sniffy, while angry and decent citizens threw things at him. One of those people was the vacationing Martina Strood.

Gibson was interviewed a hundred times.

"I bought Sniffy at a pet store," he said, holding the little rodent to his face and neck. "I figure his execution for the sake of art is a lot better than the fate awaiting his brothers and sisters. People take them home to feed to their big snakes."

Gibson said that after the performance he would frame the canvas and auction the splattered Sniffy as a prize piece for some collector's wall.

I can't remember what happened to Sniffy. My guess is that he wound up inside a snake.

I don't know how many poems were written about Sniffy. But I do know that just about all of them were better than Neruda's poem about his dead dog:

> *Yes, I believe in a heaven for all dogdom*
> *where my dog waits for my arrival*
> *waving his fan-like tail in friendship.*

The only good thing I can say about that poem is that it is better than Neruda's ode in praise of Joseph Stalin.

Rock music, which always takes a while to catch up to poetry and painting and serious music, began to feature leather-wearing guys holding a guitar in one hand and a bat or some such thing in the other. The idea was that the guy was going to express his rebellion against society by eating the bat's head right there on stage while his companions were bringing it all home in the key of G. Snakes were popular for a while, too.

Now, usually you will not find many poetry-reading people among the workers and supporters of the SPCA. They tend, like most people, to have more experience of movies than they do of books, so the credits of movies began to maintain that no animals had been harmed in the making of the film. One of the wags who had started the Jack Verge Death Count made a similar claim in a couple of his poetry collections.

The YMCA had been all over the Sniffy case, of course, because Sniffy had made it onto the television news. When Horace Semple came out with his long narrative poem called *Monkey Shredder* a few weeks after Sniffy had disappeared from the front page of section 2, and started reciting it at spoken word contests in bars all over downtown Toronto, at least one young SPCA worker took notice.

This was Dodie Mayhew, who spent most of her working days travelling to decrepit barns and stinking bungalows to gather dead and dying cats and dogs from interior spaces almost filled with old newspapers and animal dung. She wore a fabric badge on her upper arm and a gauze mask on her lower face. That's what she wore at work, and that's what she wore the first time she went to hear Horace Semple recite.

This was at the Old Country Tavern just west enough from the Annex to qualify as authentic. There was a room upstairs for poetry and a room downstairs for the regulars, and when the poets were reading or reciting upstairs the people at the back of the room could hear the cue ball hitting some other ball downstairs. The upstairs room had its own facilities, and it had that kind of darkness you achieve by having lots of softly glowing beer ads and not much else in the way of illumination. It made for comfy poetry, usually, and encouraged anonymous heckling from the audience in the five rows of straight-backed chairs.

Dodie Mayhew was, on the occasion we are interested in, sitting on an end chair of the third row, a pint of India Pale Ale in one hand and a dead common marmoset in the other. This hand, monkey and all, was inside a big pocket in her poacher's jacket. She hooted along with everyone else after the MC finished his introduction of Horace Semple. She sipped her ale while Semple stood, book open in his hand, only occasionally consulting it or turning a page. *Monkey Shredder* does not feature any common marmosets, but then on the other hand, no poacher's jacket would have pockets big enough for the kind of monkeys that came to grief in Semple's verses.

The poet was not going to be able to recite the whole poem, thank goodness. As I recall hearing, Horace got about half way through his allotted time, when he heard someone shout from the darkened audience.

"Ansasen!"

I have no idea why she shouted a word in Haitian creole. Anyway, the poem came to an end. Then a little dead monkey hit Horace Semple on the knee and fell in a sprawl in front of his feet, with which the poet stepped backward.

Chairs scraped, people bumped into one another in the gloom, and poetry was over for the night. Some people took the time to drain their beer glasses and banged the empties on the bar. Others jostled at the top of the stairs. The poet, though a step back from the spot on which he had been standing, was still in the light, and beside him was a woman in a poacher's jacket, holding a digital camera at arm's length and immortalizing the pair's propinquity.

Then she went and took her place in the unruly crowd at the top of the stairs. The young bartender had often watched on television as men in galoshes retrieved an octopus from the ice during a break in a Toronto-Chicago hockey game, but he had never imagined that he would have to figure out how to get a dead monkey off a bar room floor.

You can see where this is going, I think.

Yes, indeed, for a few months, every time Horace Semple tried to recite his long poem, a dead hamster or expired white rat would land at his feet. No matter how carefully the bouncers checked the people coming into the bar on poetry night, a disguised Dodie Mayhew would get in and sneak a small cadaver with her. First they checked for poacher's jackets, but Dodie was ready for them. She would come in with a book bag or with her arm in a sling, and halfway through the recital she would shout.

"Moordenaar!"

And there would be an animal's corpse, though not often a monkey, on the stage.

Of course there were copycat dead-animal-pitchers at

readings all over the country for a few months, but in many cases the protesters did not seem to understand the issue. Someone in Edmonton hurled a living and very angry cat at the reader, who had never written a line about an abused animal. In Vancouver some confused vegans chucked tomatoes and rutabagas, as if we were having a melodrama revival.

But Dodie Mayhew knew what she was doing. She waited for this latest fad to subside. Then she set her sights on Jack Verge.

Verge was appearing for the nth time at the Leadslingers Tavern in Hamilton, a dingy bar with worn carpets looking forlorn in the no-smoking era. This was after he had given up on haircuts, so that black ringlets with threads of white hung from his head, and a neck beard made his bare face appear surrounded by fur. He had by this time affected the work boots, twill trousers and red plaid lumberjack coat of his home region. Still, he was at least as spiffily clad as most of the people in his audience.

One of those people was not a resident of Hamilton, the city called Canada's most beautiful by David McFadden in the olden days. This was Dodie Mayhew of suburban Toronto, dressed for the evening in some kind of robe that seemed to suggest a melding of ancient Hellas and the current Middle East. The reason she was wearing such garb had little to do with religion, though her campaign did suggest some form of devotional discipline. The robe was mainly there to disguise the fact that there were animal remains affixed to her body.

Verge had recently published a book in which there was

a one-page poem titled "Bag of Puppies," a lyrical recount-
ing, apparently, of a moment in his childhood when he was
charged with the task of river bridge population control. The
reading at the Leadslingers Tavern was one stop on his tour
to promote the book. So far he had performed at six or eight
bars, arousing hoots and whistles and boot-stompings from
his fans, sometimes called the Vergers, and there had been
one review in the *Timmins Times*, in which it was pointed
out that the Verge family were pioneers in the South Porcupine area.

Apparently Dodie had a specific aim for this visit to Steel-
town. She sat quietly as the Vergers applauded poems about
diseased horses and freezing street urchins, and even smiled
once when the unshaven local beside her said, "That's real
poetry, eh?" And sure enough, at last it came time for "Bag
of Puppies," which, it turned out, is what the SPCA lady had
concealed under her robe. Not a burlap bag, as was favoured
by tardy canine birth-controllers, but a transparent plastic
sack. This sack landed before the poet's boots, with a number of little clunks that could be heard clearly in the sudden
silence that occurred in the Leadslingers Tavern. That silence formed a nice context for Dodie's shout.

"Katil!"

It did not matter whether there was a Turk in the place.
By now the stories about Dodie Mayhew were common cur-
rency in the Canadian poetry world. Nevertheless, everyone
seemed stunned. You might have expected the poet's fans to
rush the woman in the robe. You might have expected the
poet to use his work boots to kick the sack of dead dogs back

toward the pitcher. But these things did not happen. All eyes were on the man under the reading light. He stood still and straight, and his shiny ringlets hung in a tangle. Down his cheek and into his black and white beard, masculine tears flowed their crooked way.

At last he spoke. He shouted.

"You don't see! You don't see! You don't, ah, god damn it, you don't see!"

I was there. At that moment I got it. I thought back to the suicide poems Jack Verge would sometimes tuck into a volume, but which he never recited aloud. I didn't know definitively whether they were orgiastic and maudlin and intended to be romantic, but I now knew how they were connected to all these dead animal poems. I knew how they related to all the pummelled women poems. And I knew that Jack Verge was right. Dodie Mayhew didn't see. She was the SPCA lady. She loved her animals, but she didn't know how to be them.

Professor Minaccia

You know this one. The teacher is a well-dressed and really good-looking woman in her early forties. The student is a young man in jeans and a motorcycle T-shirt, not overly bright and not much used to reading books. He's in first-year university, so he has to pass an English course. The course is not all that demanding, especially for anyone who can read without holding his finger under the words. But this fellow has never had much patience for books. He spent high school with a football never more than an arm's reach away. He didn't make the university football team, but he takes his football to meals, where he usually eats with his cap on his head and his arms on the table.

This is what he says to the teacher when it is his turn to talk to her in her office: "I'll do anything to pass this course."

As if she has never heard this before. She gives her usual answer.

"Can you read *À la recherche du temps perdu* by the end of next semester?"

"Purdue . . . " was the response.

"You probably know it better as *Remembrance of Things Past.*"

"I don't think . . . "

"Or even better, *In Search of Lost Time.*"

His brow was beginning to be knitted. He started to feel hope cascading away, and even a slight hint that she might be making fun of him. He could usually get past such feelings by flexing a tit muscle or giving his Wilson Super Bowl XL a smack.

But then she stopped smiling, looked blank for a few seconds, then smiled again, but this time with a touch of the genuine. She put her elbows on her desktop, put her pretty PhD chin in her hands, and looked him deep into his eye.

"You can move in with me," she said.

Here was the deal. She would give him extra tutoring in English 106: Fiction of the Modern World and show him how to use the library. He would do the grocery shopping, do the laundry, fix things, load and unload the dishwasher, and clean up after meals. She would do the cooking, and two women from the Third World would come in once a week to do the cleaning.

Good thing, too, because it was a big house: four bedrooms,

four bathrooms, a huge living room that opened onto a huge deck and hot tub out front overlooking the inlet. He got the bedroom farthest from the ocean and farthest from hers, which also opened onto the deck. She was a little more than twice his age, but seemed to take for granted that he would entertain no ideas about hanky-panky.

Still, his moving in was her idea.

Here was another part of the deal. He wasn't allowed to have any visitors at the house. He wasn't allowed to bring his Wilson to the dining room table. That's where she would do the tutoring. He would load the dishwasher and clear the table, and then they would open their books.

At the university she dressed modern but splendid: silk shirts, black Anita Pallenberg pantsuits, and shoes from the Via Montenapoleone. But as soon as she got home she dropped her black Caran d'Ache briefcase and went straight to her bedroom, straight into her walk-in closet, and back out in her kick-around-home apparel, often some three-hundred-dollar jeans and a white shirt with the collar turned up, sometimes a dress whose hem flew about and revealed her bare legs. Very good bare legs.

If he was home from school, he would be fixing the grout in the guest shower, or putting away the lovely things he had brought from the bakery on Fourth Avenue. He had headphones on so that he could listen to gangsta rap, even while she had Poulenc on in three rooms. If she happened to be in the mood, and especially if it was Friday, she would invite him to have a drink with her, in the living room or on the deck. She never asked him what he would like. He would like a beer, no glass. She would give him whatever she was having, a glass of Saint Chinian, often.

You're thinking about the laundry. Obviously, most of her clothes were going to go to a high-end dry cleaner, and a lot of the laundry consisted of dish towels and bedsheets and so on. Once in a while one of her T-shirts would show up in the basket, some socks, stuff she wore at the gym. But no undergarments. His guess was that she either handwashed them at her sink, or maybe threw them away after one wearing. He ironed everything, including the T-shirts and the sheets. The sheets. She slept on a king-size bed, so the sheets were not all that easy to iron, but he got better and better at it. Sometimes he would hold a sheet to his face and enjoy the scent of the dryer. 320-count Egyptian cotton. No silk. She wore silk pajamas, he knew, because sometimes on a Sunday morning she would be wearing them under a matching housecoat, drinking coffee and doing the *New York Times* crossword. She would save them during the week to do them quickly on Sunday morning. But she never saved the crosswords from Monday, Tuesday, and Wednesday. Too easy. He was welcome to try those ones, after he had done all his assigned reading.

Now he knew the capital of Yemen.

On his early-semester essay about *Jane Eyre* he got a C+. She didn't grade it; one of her teaching assistants did, the one he had his seminar with. This was a little asshole with pimples. Asked him to leave his football on the floor during class. He went to his English seminar on Tuesday afternoons, and that was the day when their schedules clicked, meaning that he would get a ride home in her BMW Z4 Roadster. If it wasn't raining, she kept the top down, no matter the air temperature. Her hair flew and her small bony hand on the gearshift did too. On Tuesdays she wore a Pallenberg skirt suit, and when she sat down and back in that BMW leather, her knees were there and then some.

Keep your eyes on the road, he told himself. As if that would save him just in case.

"I notice that a lot of your stuff is European," he shouted one Tuesday afternoon—shouted because they were going fast, downhill, against the wind.

"You're not," she shouted.

But I am not part of her stuff, he thought.

"My husband was born in Europe," she said. "We have a house in Italy."

Had, he thought.

Because he knew this much: her husband was dead, had been dead for five years. You would say he was lucky to know that. One day early in the semester, he was walking home with some stuff from the drugstore when he met the neighbour lady just coming out through her wrought-iron gate. A nice-looking woman, maybe fifty-five, with a two-hundred-dollar hairdo.

"You must be the boy who's just moved in next door," she said, kindly but with a laugh behind it.

"I'm not related or anything," he said. "I just work here— there."

"Oh, I know. We have lived here for decades. We never really got to know the late Mr. Minaccia, but we do know that he might as well be alive."

"What?"

But she was already getting into a taxicab that had appeared without a sound.

His English teacher had not finished teaching him how to conduct research, so he did what he always did when he needed some information. He had a beer with his friend Adam. Adam carried or bounced a basketball wherever he went, as for instance to the Dog and Dog Pub, where he was to be found this afternoon.

"You are talking about Guido Minaccia," said Adam. "You want to stay away from him." Unlike his friend, Adam read the newspaper every day.

"He's dead."

"He might as well be alive," said Adam.

The conversation never did get more specific than that, but they had been friends since elementary school, so he and Adam had a couple more beers and some heavily salted snacks, and talked about everything young men like to talk about, and you pretty well know what that might be. Finally, Adam offered some advice, though he never explained the knowledge on which he had based it.

"Look around for a black Cadillac Escalade parked in the neighbourhood. See if there is a guy sitting in it with the engine off."

Using a hot tub back east is pretty well a winter thing, but in Vancouver you don't mind getting into that nearly-too-hot water any time of the year, even when it is raining. The widow Minaccia didn't have much time to sit around getting blanched, what with all the marking and class preparation her job foisted on her, but she did like to put in a half-hour from time to time. There was none of that bare naked stuff—she always wore her little black two-piece OYE swimsuit. And there was no question of sharing. She told him that he could use the hot tub for half an hour when she wasn't home, and he was not allowed onto the deck when she was soaking. He was, however, quick enough once in a while to catch a glimpse of her stepping into the tub—or she was slow enough.

Even without her Milan shoes her legs looked long and trim, he figured. That was the word, trim. Then she was a head of expensive hair above the hot water, the North Shore Mountains and the Islands in the background. He finished putting the dishes away and opened *The Mill on the Floss*.

As for the Escalade, that took care of itself. One evening he was walking along their street, protecting his paper bag of vegetables from a tender rain. Half a block from their gate some headlights flicked on and off, and there was the hulking SUV on the side street. He was meant to walk over and say hello at the open driver's window.

"Did you want to talk to me?" he asked, trying not to sound like a young football tough.

"Your name's Michael, right?" said the guy sitting there. A very short stubble on his lower face, about the same on his skull.

"Yes. I heard about you."

"Oh, really? You heard about me? That's nice. You heard about me."

The idea being that he was a dangerous man, so don't make any mistakes. There was a whiff of some body perfume, maybe the kind that the football boy used to wear.

"You know I'm working for Mrs. Minaccia."

"*Doctor*."

"Sorry?"

"It's *Doctor*. Minaccia. Something worth remembering, Michael."

There was an awkward silence, as could be expected, and which the guy in the Cadillac didn't mind at all. Then he explained some things to the young university student. The man in the black suv with the beads of rain on its roof would always be there, watching the house, making sure of something no one else needed to know about.

"And Michael?" he said before zipping the window up.

"Yes, sir?"

"I'm not a sir, Michael."

"Oh. Yes?"

"Remember that you are a college student and a handyman. That's all you are. If you see the lady doing something that makes you interested in a certain way, you are strong enough to keep hold of yourself, aren't you, Michael."

"Yes, sir. Yes—"

And up zipped the window, lickety-split.

"I've finished *Swann's Way*," he said.

They were sitting at the dining room table while she explained the problem of comma splices, sometimes called run-on sentences.

"What?"

"I looked it up, and there's no way even *you* could read *À la research—*"

"*Recherche.*"

"Even *you* couldn't read that by the end of the school year."

"We could argue about that," she said. "But how did you like it?"

"I don't much care about a guy that has to get his mother to sleep with him at night."

"I may or may not agree," she said, and she appeared to have allowed the smile that showed her very white teeth. "But what about the way he handles memory, the *recherche?*"

"Okay, I thought the business about that sponge cake was pretty good."

"Madeleine."

"My father used to sing a song called 'Paddlin' Madeleine Home'"

"Be careful," she said.

Everyone has the same advice, he thought.

The reason he had told the lady professor that he would do anything to get through her course really did not have much to do with her looks. He said that because her teaching assistant had assigned him an F grade on the in-class essay they had written during the first week. He had never received an F in high school. In fact, he had always received a B. The reason for this was that in high school you would get a passing grade if you could figure out how to make marks with your pen. Or turn on a flashlight.

Okay, an F, but she had said that that essay would not count on the final grade. It was supposed to give you an idea of the distance you had to cover. I will do anything, he thought. Now the first semester was almost half over, and he had earned a C for his first take-home exam. When Dr. Minaccia handed back the exams, no one was looking at him in a funny way. Except for Adam, his friend Adam.

Well, Adam knew. He had to tell someone, as the old saying goes, so he had told his friend Adam. About everything except the guy in the Escalade.

"Looks like she has a nice ass," said Adam, who was carrying his Wilson. "She got a nice ass?"

"It's not like that," he said. "I do the dishes. She helps me with the texts. You won't get it, but I'm starting to like Joseph Conrad."

Adam gave him a long look that was meant to convey mature analysis.

"Where's your football?" he asked.

Fiction of the Modern World was not the only thing she taught him. As time went by he learned how to fold freshly ironed sheets properly, how to pour a glass of Nebbiolo, what he was allowed to stand on when it came time to clean the high windows looking onto the deck. One day he came home from some errands downtown and found ten new pairs of Italian socks on his bed. A quick opening of his sock drawer showed that he was no longer in possession of the socks that had survived high school.

"Thank you for the socks," he said at dinner. "Really."

"What size shoe do you wear?"

For some reason he could feel his face flush. He thought that it was time to change the subject.

"I have started to read *Within a Budding Grove*—"

"We will take the shoes out of your wages," she said, sounding a little as if she were in a classroom

"But you don't—"

"That is good about *Within a Budding Grove*."

Next day in the car they discussed the question of European colonialism in the fiction of Joseph Conrad, and when they got to the house they both went and took care of some chores. He had just reached the main floor with a basket full of warm sheets and was turning to go upstairs when he saw her in the kitchen, pouring two glasses of Nebbiolo. She was wearing her two-piece swimsuit and patent leather high-heeled sandals.

"You can fold those sheets later," she said. "Take them upstairs and change into your swimsuit."

He couldn't believe the beating of his heart as he hurried upstairs. Behind him he could hear the clacking of her shoes on the tiles. He did manage to get his clothes off and his trunks on, but he had never been so clumsy at doing so.

This is ridiculous, he told himself, maybe in his head, maybe in a whisper. Shut up, he told himself immediately after that, and grabbed a warm towel on his way downstairs.

Don't knock over that glass of wine, he told himself, in his head for sure, as he approached the hot tub. There was slanted sunlight on the deck, but the tub was in the shade. He eased himself down into the hot, hot water, trying to think of an apt quip and failing to do so.

He looked across the inlet toward the dark mountains. He looked back toward the sliding glass doors to see whether they were open or closed or whatever they were supposed to be.

He could not look at her face and shoulders he knew to be above the swirling water, but he could see what was below the surface, blurry as it all was. A black swimsuit and long white legs.

Finally she spoke, and he had to look up at her face. He had no idea what she had said.

What he told himself was: don't even think of accidentally touching legs.

He had to admit that his new shoes were the most comfortable shoes he had even worn, including sneakers. These ones were heavy enough that he got a satisfying little impact when he walked on the sidewalk, but they were light enough that all the bones in his body felt the connections they were supposed to feel. If anyone asked, if Adam asked, he would never be able to describe the feeling. He did not tell Adam about the hot tub, and for good reason. The box the shoes came in said Berluti.

"So, what's the latest?" asked Adam. They had met just outside the fancy food store on Fourth.

"I'm about a quarter of the way through *The Guermantes Way*. I think that's how you say it."

"You know what I mean, Asshole. How are things going with the mobster's widow?"

"Not really mobster, Adam. And I got a B- on my midterm essay."

"You are the slowest, stupidest best friend I ever had, Soupy. It is very clear to me that the lady is a widow, a fox-like widow, a cougar, as they say, who would like to—"

"Make up your mind on the animal life, Adam."

Adam let him take three steps in his Berluti loafers.

"Okay, as your best friend and lifetime mentor, I am going to give you a piece of information that may make the remainder of your life a little more likely to afford you some knowledge and self-esteem. The lady would like it better if you were not a little field mouse or other diminutive prey of the hovering falcon."

"Oh, now she's a bird."

"I am just sayin', Soupy, you will never see a proper relationship if she has to make all the moves."

That statement gave him a lot of trouble in his head while he walked home with four small white bags partly filled with nearly perfect pieces of fruit. He was thinking so hard that he was surprised by the voice.

"Nice shoes, Sport."

It was the guy in the Escalade. He was not really *in* the Escalade, but rather standing beside it and smoking a cigarette.

"Thanks."

"Don't get wise, Sport."

"I wasn't. I was just a million miles away."

"Good idea. But I don't get to make those decisions. I would like to offer a bit of advice, though."

Like everyone else, he thought.

"Shoot!" No, wrong choice of word!

"Always know where the nearest door is," said the guy with the cigarette.

Ever since he had been invited to share the hot tub, he had been able to look her in the face, either in the water or at the table. When she drove him home from school he could look at her profile without averting his gaze, as they say. He had even found it possible to look at her legs, the way they became more visible when she sat down in the BMW's driver's seat. Contrary to his earlier remarks to his friend Adam, he now found her to be a great pleasure to look at. She must have been aware of his gaze. She must have been a person who had grown used to the male gaze. The male gaze: it was a phrase that had come up in more than one class, including the ones about *Tess of the D'Urbervilles.*

One day he found a pair of her underpants in the laundry basket. As if it had got there by accident. He wondered. Here was something he might mention to Adam, or he might not. Well, he would not mention it. Unmentionables, that's what his father had called such things in jest, pretending to be older and more formal than he was. He could not ask her whether he should go ahead and include them in the wash. He just did. But before that, (you know what's coming) he gave them a little sniff. No one was going to see. You know that ninety-nine young men out of a hundred would do that in his circumstances. Not that there were many in his cir- cumstances.

Did she do it on purpose? That's what he wondered. He did not mention it, just put the laundered item on her bed while putting away the ironed sheets and dishtowels and the like. And no, he did not iron the unmentionables.

Adam could say anything he wanted to. He didn't know that much about the guy in the Escalade. Go ahead, make your move, Adam could advise. Sure. I'd like to see what you would do, he thought.

Maybe he should give her a hug one morning when she went off to her office and he headed for the student union. That's what everyone did these days. But no, she was still a professor and he was a B- student. And her late husband's employees were still, it seemed, employed.

It had been quite a while since he'd carried his football around. In fact, he was not sure where it might be, proba- bly under his bed, or in the back of his clothes closet. He was the person who vacuumed around such places, but he could not remember.

Instead of a football, he carried a book wherever he went. Well, students did that, carried bags with books in them. But even when he was nowhere near the university, he had a book in his hand. Sometimes it was a novel he was reading for her class, and at other times it was likely to be something in translation, Dostoyevsky, or Thomas Mann. Remember, this was a young man who had been what the librarians apparently called a "reluctant reader." One of those peculiar people who will sit for an hour in the dentist's waiting room without reading, either staring straight ahead of them or fiddling with a little phone.

Toward the end of the semester he was carrying *Cities of the Plain*, a novel he hadn't heard of a year earlier. It was and is five hundred pages long, and demands some memory from its reader. He even went back and reread some of Proust's earlier ponderings, a sure sign that he was finding reading to be enjoyable. It will not become untrue that leaping into the air and catching an oval leather ball is enjoyable. Living in an extra world, though, is a gift from the god who made people decide to write their stories down.

He was still young. At times he thought archly.

His professor, sitting at the cleared dining room table with him, actually said, "Are you sure that you should be reading French fiction instead of English fiction when the mid-year exam in the latter is a week away?"

She was smiling. Her blouse was undone a button more than usual.

Then they got to work, now with a glass of pinot noir, which he thought went well with George Eliot's sentences.

As the routine became body memory, the work became just a background to the reading and studying. A lot of nights, when he thought about the things he had seen during the day, he would go to sleep with a young man's erection. There is no getting around that sort of thing when a young man is the age he is. But becoming educated is not natural. If he had not been a student in the widow's class he might never have picked up a book without reluctance. Now when he saw the guys he used to hang with he wondered how they could just go along in their unamplified lives. He still kept track of the football scores, the only kind of reading he used to enjoy, but they had become a pretty small part of his life.

If, a year ago, he had heard some guy say that reading and studying books were enjoyable in themselves, he would have made a loud and probably impolite sound. For the rest of his life, to be sure, he would probably relate the pleasure of a good English sentence with the shape in a Vivienne Westwood blouse on the other side of the dining room table. But even in his biology class he was the student who knew the history of ancient Middle Eastern biology.

In the mid-year examination on late nineteenth-century fiction he got a B+.

Over the Christmas break he went to stay with his parents and sister outside a dry little town in the Interior. His mother didn't say anything about the book he carried everywhere, but she eyed him. In her expression might have been seen a little bit of concern and another little bit of hope. His father was his usual self—his eyes were directed toward the television, where an ice hockey game was in progress, or to the newspaper, where the games of the previous day were described. His kid sister, a popular girl in high school politics, punched him in the shoulder and asked him where his pigskin was. He was not sure whether she was capable of a double entendre.

For Christmas Day the uncles and aunts and cousins from up the valley all arrived and filled the house with old stories and noisy children. Two tables were pushed together, and a kids' table set to one side. The Christmas tree lights became highly visible when darkness claimed the windows. The immense turkey glinted like copper, and tiny wine glasses stood in front of some of the celebrants.

"It's kind of Dickensian," he said to his mother, who had just brought the bowl of sweet potatoes from the kitchen.

"What's that, dear?" she asked, then turned to fetch the Brussels sprouts.

And so it went. During the holiday he worked days at the packing house, and at night he read his way through *The Prisoner*. He had brought with him a copy of the French text so that he could get the feeling of reading that once in a while.

"That's a thick book," his mother said one evening. They could hear the hockey announcer in the next room, telling people what was happening as if they were not watching it. "Is that for your course at university?"

"Not really," he said. "It's more like for my course at home."

"How is that working out?" She knew that he was living at a professor's house, but not that the professor was a widowed woman.

"It's a pretty good deal," he replied, looking serious and smiling at the same time.

He was glad to get back down to the coast and back into his routine. While doing the laundry, he felt that the hand-work was enjoyable, simply enjoyable. The cloth was warm in his hands. His hands were intelligent and quick, but in no hurry. There were no metaphors to make about this fold-ing and ironing. It was just pleasant, in a way that pushing a hand truck at the packing house was not.

"How was your Christmas with your family?" she asked while they were having a cappuccino after dinner and be-fore he would clear the table.

"I couldn't wait to get back here," he said, without shy-ness.

"How sweet!" And she blew an air kiss. A kind of Italian thing, one would guess.

So he was distracted for a little while as they started their mini-seminar about the English novel and what traces of the romantic movement could still be found in it as the twenti-eth century came around. But then there was Joseph Con-rad, and the discussion was just so damned interesting. There was still a beautiful woman in wonderful modish clothing across the table, and her voice with its mixture of ivory and earth. But a tall wooden ship creaked in the wind, and he had to know what Conrad had done with his sen-tences to take him there.

Three hours slipped past, though they usually stopped after half that time. This evening there were two glasses of Mandurian Primitivo beside the hot tub. He could not dis-cern the line between physical comfort and intellectual hap-piness for a long time, as the jets of hot air nudged his body.

He sipped the big raisiny wine, and then as he saw how she treated it, he glugged some. He was in the moving water with a woman who knew everything, and yet he suspected that if she felt such a whim she could make him disappear from the lives of everyone who knew him.

After about fifteen dreamy minutes, while more and more lights came on across the inlet, he saw that her breasts beneath the bubbling water were bare. And barely visible, as the only light anywhere near them was coming from a dimmed chandelier in the living room.

After another ten minutes or so, she drained her glass and stepped out of the tub, her back to him, and left footprints on the deck as she disappeared into the dark. He stayed in the water and played with the word "darkness" in his silent mind.

They did not go to the hot tub every night. Perhaps once a week. Each time, though, he thought about that lack of clarity and how he would describe it if he were a novelist. But every time they sank into the bubbles, her swimsuit was there. It was something in itself, yes, something.

Every time he vacuumed the back balcony he looked for the Cadillac. It was not always parked in the same place, but it was always in sight. He could not usually see the man who drove it, because during the early part of the second semester, it was generally raining, and the guy was probably in the driver's seat, smoking with the window open a crack.

So the spring semester hurried by. Soon there would be days without heavy grey clouds, and soon the North Shore

Mountains would be fully visible right to their pointy tops. More and more bicycles would appear on the streets and outside every building at the university. Spring break came, and then ended with midterm examinations. He took the occasion to study a little, but spent most of his off-duty time reading *The Sweet Cheat Gone*, feeling anger at Albertine, and almost asking himself why Professor Minaccia had dared him to read this long book that hadn't even been written in English.

Inapt love, he had come to understand now that he was a reader, was a diamond mine for novelists and playwrights.

But despite his comparative inattention, he did as well as he had done in high school, where you could pass from grade to grade by using a sliver of your brain. In his other courses he passed quite comfortably, and in English he earned his first university A. If you can count A- as an A. As Professor Minaccia was handing the exam papers back to members of her class, she pronounced his surname wrong, just a little.

Later she gave him the night off, and he went for a beer with a few of his friends. They remarked on the fact that they had not been seeing as much of him as they had earlier done. He wished that he had brought his exam paper with him, so that he could plunk it down and tap the A- with his finger tip. On second thought, he was glad that he had not. For the rest of the evening he pretended to be more squiffed than he was, and then he went home just before midnight. The word "home" entered his head, and then he began to think about where he would go once summer arrived.

She was reading some academic journal in a living room recliner that he had never seen her use before. She was wearing a black *vestaglia* that looked like silk, the way it caught light as it seemed to spill toward the floor, and on her feet the kind of slippers a young man imagines but doesn't get to see.

"Congratulations," she said, and "good work, Mr.—", and she pronounced his surname correctly.

"Call me Michael," he said, smiling, maybe just a little squiffed.

She stood up, black fabric gleaming.

"I just stayed up to make sure you got home all right."

"Thank you."

"And as for Albertine—"

"I'm letting her go," he said.

"But stay with her author," she said, and before turning to head for the stairs, she put the palm of her small hand on his chest, for less than a second.

It was a kind of motherly, professorial kind of touch, he told himself, as he checked the refrigerator and wrote out a list of groceries to buy tomorrow. But it was as if he could feel her hand on his chest still, though it could not have been there for more than half a second, that touch. Then he thought of how much he liked being a reader now, and even how much he liked getting an essay together, even if he did wind up writing something that a thousand other under-graduates had written at the same school. Then he thought of the guy sitting in the suv around the corner.

I mean, think about it. There were definite signs that she

was thinking about something other than being a boss or a professor, or if not thinking, something. A wardrobe gesture here, a touch there, a few words. But yes, but then she went to her room. Adam would have said that he was supposed to follow and find out what would happen, and if nothing, well, there is always nothing.

But no, there was no use thinking along those lines. There were a lot of people who knew where he was living and would make assumptions. They did not know enough. They may have heard very faintly about certain things that Vito Minaccia was said to have done. But they didn't know about the guy in the black Escalade. Same colour as most of her European clothes. She was, he could not help thinking, beautiful in mourning.

Is there some kind of colour that resembles lavender but is still a shimmer of green? That was the colour of her BMW, and as he polished the surface, feeling the wax disappear from under his cloth, he thought that maybe that colour matched her eyes. Then he realized that he could not remember her eyes' colour, even though he had found the, what was it, nerve, to look into them

Nor could he really tell that evening, while sitting at the dining room table, the cappuccino just the right temperature. He had the text of *The Waves* open at random, and he did have a v5 Hi-Tecpoint pen more or less at the ready. She was holding her white cup in the long fingers of both hands, and wearing a black T-shirt that probably sold for two hundred dollars. He looked at her eyes, and they were part of her look of amusement.

"What is it?" she asked, lightly.

"I think I—"

"Shh," she said, and put down her white cup.

The spring semester was sliding away, and he did have to study for exams in his other courses. He was going to settle for whatever he got, though generally his grades had been rising a little. He was going to see whether he could erase the minus behind his A in English 106. But he could not let Albertine go. Or the memory of Albertine would not let him go.

So he would not begin to read the final volume. Only an idiot would start in on that long conclusive narrative when there were final exams to be faced. He had to read *Howard's End* and think about English society instead of French. He wondered why Professor Minaccia had not assigned one of Forster's Italian novels.

Maybe not lavender. Maybe a kind of cobalt with a touch of green.

And so the spring semester slid away. He thought of about a dozen similies to describe the way the semester slid away, but similies didn't seem to do the trick. Slide was enough.

He did the laundry and polished the floors and reread all his class notes and the pages and pages of notes he had taken at the dining room table. He did the grocery shopping and vacuumed the BMW and skimmed through all his textbooks. He sat down one morning and realized that a year's worth of mathematics had at last fallen nicely and snugly into some back part of his brain. He finished his essay on Virginia Woolf and turned it in on time. His English professor caught him humming a tune while wiping the stainless steel sink.

He wrote all the exams, turned in all the assignments, went to the campus pub with some of his classmates, and sprawled, just kind of sprawled as he downed a beer or two.

That night he got in a little late, and she was there to open the door for him. She was wearing the *vestaglia* and high-heeled slippers again, and when she turned to walk to the liquor cabinet, he felt sober and drunk at the same time. Now in her hands there were two small glasses of kir.

"A traditional nightcap for serious students of French literature," she said, handing him a wine glass with dark purple light in it.

"I'm, uh, a kind of serious all-around normal freshman student," he said. "I don't even understand much French."

"I think that one day you will."

"I could enroll in French next year."

It tasted sweet, with a lift out of the sweetness. Currants. He wondered whether Albertine had ever had a glass of kir with him. No, not him—

Her glass was empty already.

"I think I passed everything okay," he said.

"Of course."

"I think I might get an A in English."

"It's certainly possible," she said.

He tried to drain his glass, but it was going to take a while.

"I have to be thinking about where I can work for the summer. I'll probably go home and get work in the orchards or the packing house."

She was still holding her empty glass by the stem.

"I thought that you could stay here and work for me," she said, and for once she was not looking at him while she spoke.

"No, I—"

"Give it a thought," she said, and turned to go, her wine glass still in her hand. As she did so, the tip of her breast, or the viscous material covering her breast, touched his upper arm.

Before he went to bed that night he stripped down to his new briefs and drained the hot tub, then spent an hour wiping it clean. He left it empty to dry and left the cover leaning on its edge. Then he went to his quarters, had a shower, and lay on the top of the bedclothes until he drifted away. A copy of *The Past Recaptured* lay on his bedside table, a bookmark on top of it.

The next day he had some thinking to do, so he left the house early and walked all day. He could have done the outdoor chores and maybe some floor-cleaning inside, but he didn't want to make it look as if he had made a decision. So he walked and walked. He bought a newspaper and read it while having lunch at a cheap place. He stopped in for a beer and drank half of it over an hour at a nearly empty pub on

Broadway. He tried to make up his mind. He wished that the present were more like the past, when decisions were made and he followed them.

It was beginning to get around to dusk when he got back. Feeling indecisive still, he hesitated in the shadow of a hedge across the road from her door, and it was a good thing that he did, because he saw two men coming out that door, not turning to say anything. One of them was the guy who was usually sitting in the black suv. The other one he didn't recognize.

He walked some more, then, and waited until it got really dark before he went to the door. It wasn't all that dark there, what with the yard lights. Of course, when he got inside and closed the door quickly and for some reason quietly behind him, there she was.

In bare feet. Rayon pyjamas that could have come from a mall store in the suburbs. Her hair was up high, her white neck exposed in the back, and she did not look at all like an academic woman. Her eyes were smeary and her chin was not resolute. She was a lovely woman in her forties and he felt awful, as if he were a powerful muscular man who made people do things.

He could tell that she was finished with crying. He almost said something, but he couldn't.

In fact he was as if mesmerized. He simply stood still while without any hurry she unbuttoned his shirt and removed it from him, letting it fall to the terrazzo. Then she came close. She put her hands on his waist for balance, and then she leaned forward and kissed his right nipple. She opened her lips in a small circle and drew his nipple between them and touched it with her tongue. Then she put her mouth to his left nipple, and he felt a sharp little bite.

"Goodbye," she said, and walked quickly into the darkness somewhere.

He picked up his shirt and hiked the stairs. He did not hesitate. He did not think of going anywhere else but to his room.

There he saw a very tidy arrangement of his two suitcases, the one he had arrived with, the new one that must have had his new clothes and books in it, along with his backpack, and his football. All packed and ready to go.

He lifted everything, taking a while to see how he could do it, and edged his way sideways down the stairs. Then he had to manage the door. He hated the awkwardness of this. It shouldn't have had to be awkward. Just in time he remembered to put his house key on the little table beside the door.

And began to walk, the suitcases heavy, toward the nearest bus stop. He was glad that it wasn't raining. In the dark rainless street he had three questions go through his head. Who packed his bags? Was there anything in them that he didn't know about?

Would he finish reading the last volume of Proust?

At the bus stop, he put down all his stuff. When the bus came he picked up the bags and left the football on the bench.

Then he rode that bus somewhere, downtown, maybe. There were no raindrops on the bus windows but there was no getting away from how sad he was, this A student.

Anne

What's the buzz?

He was on the TV room telephone trying to talk with the suicidal wife of his best friend, while his own was in the
kitchen, weeping about her crazy sister and the baby her
crazy sister was getting ready to have, and their own child
was crying quietly because she had been shouted at all day
and now she was alone, turning four years old in a pair of
fashionable tots' overalls with train-engineer stripes. Here
the sentence comes to an end, but listen—if writing a story
of life is supposed to be persuasive because it is so much
like life, how can you ever have a sentence come to an end?
Well, it's not for me to ask the questions. The commercial
outfits that place advertisements in the daily newspapers
ask the questions. Or so it would seem.

Between such episodes he had gotten into the habit of
looking at young women, not undressing them in his mind's

eye as the common story has it, but just watching how their legs move under, say, a pleated skirt with a dark blue and red plaid pattern, watching, say, the way they reach their long pointed fingers up to remove a tendril of hair from in front of their eyes and hook it behind one ear, from which place it will fall free in a few seconds. That sort of thing. The way all signs of intelligence fall away from their faces when they sit on the city bus and stare at the little screens they hold in front of them.

One day, between such episodes, he went to visit his best friend. His best friend's suicidal wife was away from home. Maybe she had acquired another job, who can remember everything? After they had been talking for a while, drinking some ordinary beer from the refrigerator, his best friend told him that he had recently had his first really good sexual experience in years.

"Good for you. I am glad to hear it," he said to his best friend, who finished a glug of his beer and put the long-necked bottle down, foam coming out of it a little, before replying.

Apparently that good sexual experience had been courtesy of another crazy woman, someone his best friend's wife might or might not have known. He was reminded of the accusations his own wife had been making. Yes, it was a matter of fact that somewhat in the manner of his best friend, he had recently had pretty fair sex with another crazy woman, but his wife accused him of being somewhere else, with yet another crazy woman.

This was, wasn't it, the kind of stuff that rumours are made of, but these were not really rumours, at least as far as he and his best friend and I can see. It was not as if there were a buzz going around all their circles. Or maybe there was. If there was, I don't know anything about it, so it is unlikely that he or his best friend would have a chance to either.

"You want to talk about it?" he asked his best friend.

"Never kiss and tell," his best friend said. And he was smiling. There hadn't been enough of that lately.

How does it work?

His best friend is the real McCoy. I mean that his name is Bill McCoy, not that he would ever stoop to any obvious wordplay in conversation with any new acquaintance. But you can be sure that other people so stoop.

"Heh heh," he sometimes replied. "I see what you mean. Never thought of that. That's pretty good, that one."

And no, his best friend, the other one with a crazy wife, is not named Hatfield. It is something field, but not hat. If the time comes when it matters what his name is, we will all know. Or be apprised, as they say at meetings.

They had met at a meeting. In university. It was a meeting about the new East Asia Club, or rather the East Asian Club that someone wanted to start up. He and his best friend were not the only non-Asian-looking people there, and they were not even the only non-Asian-looking people who had been taking classes in Japanese Studies, but they were two non-Asian-looking people, call them white people, who were serious about such a club's being formed, especially Bill McCoy.

In fact so serious that when the club did get started the next semester, Bill McCoy was the inaugural president and his best friend was the inaugural vice president. None of the Asian-looking students had run for these posts. Not even Michiko Miyoshi, who happened to be a considerable part of the reason that Bill McCoy attended the meeting. In Japanese written characters, her name, like most Japanese names, was made of two *kanji*, and Bill McCoy had practised making them, not with a brush but with a ballpoint pen, which is not the ideal instrument for the writing of Chinese or Japanese characters. It doesn't work very well at all.

Bill McCoy did not have good handwriting. His best friend often wondered whether that fact had anything to do with the other fact that Bill McCoy had only one arm. The arm that he had was his left, if it is not peculiar to use that designation for a person who does not need to have one arm distinguished from the other. One could say "his arm," simply. In any case, what his best friend often wondered was this: is Bill McCoy's handwriting so bad because he was supposed to be right-handed? Having lost his right arm when he was a toddler, should he not have had a lifetime of experience as a handwriter, and should not his handwriting be as good as the average right-handed writer's? Or is he a right-handed person without a right hand?

He was interested to note that when Bill McCoy started writing *kanji*, his handwriting resembled his English-language handwriting, and it was what most readers would consider pretty bad.

Going on vacation?

If it had not been for Michiko Miyoshi, Bill McCoy probably would have gone to the University of Tokyo anyway. Bill was mainly a French major, but he had lately become interested in Japanese, as in language, culture, and womenfolk. His year as president of the East Asia Club had been a big asset for all these interests. He picked up more and more Japanese expressions, learned more Japanese art history, and eventually got his arm around Miss Miyoshi. But out of his characteristic shyness and good upbringing, he did not try to take advantage of the pretty little exchange student.

"Do you know what you are getting into?" his best friend asked him one evening after a club meeting.

"Well, nothing at the moment," he replied. Though he was shy and well-behaved, he still had an adolescent sense of humour.

So things proceeded. Bill's best friend, call him Ernest if that is important, began to make remarks about his envy, about how much he would like to have a Japanese exchange student to walk around with.

"You have girls galore," said Bill. "I don't see you doing without."

"Yeah, but it nerks me to see you getting something good that I don't have."

He was kind of kidding. But even if he was envious, he was a true friend, and was happy to see his best friend make his way in the world. So it was that he paid for the beer when it came time to celebrate the scholarship. It was the first year of the Tokyo-Vancouver language scholarship, and who knows how many students had applied for it, but it was no great surprise when the first president of the East Asia Club became the first holder of the Tokyo-Vancouver scholarship.

"Drink up. We're celebrating your great good fortune, connected as it is with your relentless scholarship," said Ernest something Field. "After all these years you have bent to your books, it is about time that you got to look about the emerging postwar Land of the Rising Sun."

"Nihon."

"I know. That's how you say Japan in Japan."

"Means the sun, where it comes from. Those two *kanji*."

"Well, this beer is sunny in disposition, and there's more where it came from." They were a little squiffed, as they used to say at such moments.

"I am drinking this stuff at your behest, you will remember," said the somewhat tipsy scholarship winner. "And I have to say—I forget what I have to say."

"Probably has to do with your great and deserved fortune concerning your travels for the next two years."

"It's not going to be hick. It's not going to be a vacation."

That seemed for certain. According to the designers of the new scholarship, the bestowee would take Japanese lessons, teach English weekly at night school, and continue his area of studies at the University of Tokyo.

And so it went. In 1960 Bill McCoy went to the crippled empire and enrolled at the French department of the University of Tokyo. Michiko Miyoshi returned to her studies at Tokyo University of Foreign Studies. Her brother Akira Miyoshi was a classmate of Bill McCoy in his French classes. While Michiko disappeared into the giant tangled city that was still rebuilding fifteen years after it had been bombed to rat shit by B-29s, Bill started seeing a lot of her brother. Akira was two years older than Bill, and his French was just as good, which was not surprising, given that he had studied at the Paris Conservatory.

Bill McCoy was a pretty good amateur singer, and if he had owned a right hand, he would likely have played an instrument adequately, but his best friend in Japan had been a child prodigy at the keyboard even while his uncle had commanded troops that invaded Hong Kong and placed Bill's uncle, among other Canadian soldiers, in a most unpleasant concentration camp and fed him occasionally with low-grade rice speckled with insects and their progeny.

Nevertheless, in that very first semester at the University of Tokyo, Bill sat many an afternoon with Akira while they worked together on the latter's first important orchestral work that they together named *Trois mouvements symphoniques*.

Best dressed?

Akira Miyoshi was Japanese all right, but he was also European. I mean, his music was European music produced by a person who had grown up in Tokyo and did not have a supratarsal epicanthic fold over either eye. He had his hair cut in the European way, and wore clothes such as those a young Frenchman with artistic talent might wear. Usually he wore a black suit that accented the slimness of his body, but sometimes, at parties, for example, he wore wide-wale corduroy trousers, a jersey with wide horizontal stripes, and a black beret. He smoked his cigarettes in a long holder made of horn.

Bill McCoy, on the other hand, had no sense of fashion whatever. Before he left home his mother had always chosen his clothing, and after he had gone away to be a student, he didn't see the point of buying any clothing unless he was going to a new climate or unless a pair of trousers, say, developed a hole that got too big to be ignored. The Japanese students who were his classmates at the University of Tokyo considered him to be an eccentric *hakujin* because the only ones they had had any experience with were u.s. soldiers and sailors who were impeccable in their uniforms, even when they were staggering drunk.

He wrote aerograms home to his best friend Ernest something Field, in which he portrayed himself as a tall clumsy white guy who presented danger to delicate Japanese furniture and paper walls. Bill and his best friend, all through their lives, prized humour in their personal communications. In later life they both rued the fact that Bill McCoy had somehow lost the packet of aerograms that Ernest had mailed to him between 1960 and 1962. Bill did remember that one of his favourite moments came at the end of a typewritten aerogram, where Ernest had typed, "I must sign off now," and then written in ballpoint pen, "Yours, Off."

But in the early sixties they were an amusing pair, Akira the composer, short and slim in his suit and tie and shiny leather shoes, and Bill McCoy, tall and a little ungainly in trousers with round legs and a jacket whose sleeve left one hairy wrist visible. If you had been in a rehearsal room at the University of Tokyo on January 25th of 1961, you might have overheard these two friends singing: They sang little bits in Japanese, then little bits in French, and sometimes little bits in English.

"You have a nice tenor voice," said Akira Miyoshi in Japanese.

"But we are writing for soprano," said Bill McCoy in French.

"We should send for my sister," said Akira Miyoshi in French.

"Can she sing?" asked Bill McCoy.

"No, but I think that you have a think for her," said Akira M. in English.

"*Thing*. Not think. Thing," said Bill McCoy in English. "And maybe, just maybe I have a little thing for your sister."

They were just starting to compose songs in French for a soprano to be accompanied by a piano, Akira's favoured instrument. For these they were translating four poems by Chika Sagawa, who had died just after Akira had been born and just before Bill had. Chika Sagawa was a wonderful young surrealist poet from Hokkaido, who had flourished in a Tokyo group led by the great Kitasono Katue.

Even I have heard of Kitasono Katue. If you went to our university in those days, and if you read anything, you would end up reading Japanese poets and fiction writers. Kitasono was difficult in Japanese and less difficult in English, they say. I don't know about Chika Sagawa. Were her *quatre poèmes pour soprano et piano* difficult in French and English? You would have to read them and decide for yourself.

Are Finn and Rachel an on- and off-screen couple?

Okay, there is a clue here. These people would seem to be screen actors, either on television or, less likely, in movies. As far as I am aware, this would appear to be a dead end, or as they say in French a *cul de sac*, or as they say in Japanese, 行き止まりの通り, 行き止まりになっている通り.

I know a few Finns, and I know a couple of people named Finn. One is a mascot clown for an ice hockey team, and the other is a toddler son of a friend on an island. I know a few more Rachels, but none of them screen stars. So forget those people.

Were Bill McCoy and Michiko Miyoshi on- and off-campus lovers? I mean in 1960 or 1961?

A half century later, I mean here a couple of days ago, I emailed McCoy and asked what he could remember of Akira Miyoshi and Chika Sagawa. McCoy emailed back with the news that the names were vaguely familiar. He did remember Michiko Miyoshi.

Then his best friend wrote to ask: "Were you and Michiko lovers in Tokyo?"

He emailed back: "Define 'lovers.'"

Whats-his-field emailed back an hour later: "Did she leave her *geta* outside your door overnight?"

McCoy emailed back next morning: "I made a few extra *yen* as her French tutor."

His best friend emailed immediately: "Did I ask such an intimate question?"

What we are getting here is the faintly discernible outlines of the first act in a modern *kabuki* play. These are usually based on sad romances that have recently been discussed in the tabloid newspapers and on television. Probably nowadays they first show up on what are called for some reason social networking sites on the Internet. Thank goodness there were no cellphones in 1961. Or if there had been, maybe it would have been a more complicated job to build the Berlin Wall. But that is another postwar story.

In any case, usually these modern *kabuki* are about sad young lovers who commit suicide by jumping off high buildings or in front of trains.

The great founder of *kabuki* in the seventeenth century was Chikamatsu. One has to wonder whether Chika Sagawa chose her name in memory of the great playwright of suicide. She was only twenty-five when she died, of stomach cancer, apparently. When she was a girl in Hokkaido her name had been Aiko Kawasaki.

Chika doesn't seem to mean anything interesting.

Chikamatsu died at the age of seventy-two, of natural

causes. Remember that he made stylized theatre from real-life suicides. Once he said, "Art is something that lies in the slender margin between the real and the unreal."

You may assume that Bill McCoy and Michiko Miyoshi did lie down in that slender margin. Or that Bill McCoy and his suicidal wife have kind of made up or are kind of made up. Usually off-screen.

Brown in ring?

Bill McCoy was in Japan for two years, and while he was there he became unexpectedly interested in *sumo*, or as it is called in North America, sumo wrestling. Having been around Japanese stuff ever since leaving his little home village in the Okanagan Valley and moving to Vancouver, he knew that there was some connection between *sumo* and the music he heard at the *kabuki* theatre. Maybe it had something to do with Zen, the contradictory slice of philosophy and behaviour that pleased cultural tourists so much because it didn't seem to involve much work. But how unlike, at first, the meaty crash of naked giants and the disappearing notes of a garden flute. No, *sumo* came from Shinto, the ancient religion that grew out of the country's immeasurably old rocks, upon which humans fought with divine spirits.

At first, sitting a few metres from the *dohyō*, Bill was alarmed by the clothing, the belt or whatever that was, that allowed great expanses of male skin to be seen, that looked as if a high kick or a firm grab could dislodge that wrapped silk and expose—he did not want to see whatever that would be, whether the greatly pendulous or the dark nether canal.

But he became, especially when supported by some mysterious oriental beer, a mostly ignorant aficionado, if it is all right to leap to the Spanish ring from the Nihonese. Bill McCoy had never been an athletic boy, did not even know what eight cities were in the National League. But sitting with Akira Miyoshi facing the *sumo* ring, he gazed intently as a huge man threw a handful of salt before him, and he cocked an ear to hear whether the young composer beside him was whispering any inspired notes.

After the elaborate ancient rituals had been performed, each match might be over in a few seconds, but even Bill McCoy understood that each of those seconds had lived since the Islands of Japan had risen from the sea.

The *hakujin* knew that everything in Japan was portentous, though this might not be true for the Japanese.

McCoy wondered whether something like that was true for the wife he took home with him from Japan.

"Does this country seem mysterious to you?" he asked her in Japanese fifteen years after they had settled into a small house twenty blocks from the school he taught French and Spanish in.

"I live in a mysterious place," she replied. "When I was a girl I lived in a country that was trying to become like this one. Now I see that soon this one will not be able to keep up with that one."

"I like them both," he said. "But I hope that they will always be different."

"What about Akira's music?" she asked. "One time it is French. The next time it is Japanese. What if he finds a way to join them?"

"I like it better the way it is now. I like to have two musics."

"I have two countries," she said. "But they are both mysterious."

"Is that a Zen Buddhist remark?" he asked. He still had not retired from his effort to add humour to her life.

"I know nothing about Zen Buddhism," she said. "I am a Catholic."

Bill McCoy told his best friend that he wondered how Japanese Catholics felt about *kabuki*, what with its reliance on suicide.

Is Taylor made for the big time?

In the first decade of the twentieth century, a ferociously talented composer named Samuel Coleridge-Taylor never stopped working, perhaps sensing that he would drop dead at the age of thirty-seven. The few who heard his work called him Mahler. They called him Elgar. They called him Dvořák.

They also called him bastard. And they called him nigger. He was a young Englishman brought up by his mother and her father. His own father went back to Africa without knowing that he had a son. In 1910, two years before he died, Samuel Coleridge-Taylor wrote a cantata for chorus and or-

chestra called *A Tale of Old Japan*, Op.76. The libretto was
a poem by Alfred Noyes, who published a new edition of the
poem in book form in 1914. In his introduction to the ele-
gant little volume, Noyes wrote of Taylor's composition: "He
preserved every cadence of every line, and yet he gave the
freedom of music to the whole, in a way that poets had
ceased to think possible. It is therefore to his memory that
I would dedicate the poem, all too poor a chrysalis as it must
seem for those exquisite wings."

At the end of the poem the young painter Sawara finally
bursts the "golden gate" and becomes a great artist. A hundred years and then some later, we might say that he was
ready for the big time.

But here is what Bill McCoy's best friend liked to picture:
McCoy sitting with his friend Akira Miyoshi fifty years after
Opus 76 was first performed, listening to the great chorus
streaming music from continent to continent, absorbing the
London musician's breath, feeling his heart beat against
their lungs, knowing without telling one another that art was
the place for sharp sadness, not the precipice.

"Does it sound Japanese to you?" asked Bill McCoy.

"Well, as you know, I lived for a while in France, and I
know that I was there half a century after that music, that
era, but maybe we can say that it sounds like the Japanese
that people in Paris were taken by at the turn of the century."

"The Floating World."

"Exactly," said Akira.

He lifted the stylus and played the last few minutes of

Taylor's favourite composition again. When it came to an end he lifted the stylus and put it on its rest. He flicked a speck of dust off the right arm of his French suit. Then the two of them endured a little Japanese silence, as best they could in the huge city.

"When you were in Paris," said the white young man, "did you have any interesting romantic adventures?"

"By romantic, do you mean erotic?" asked the Japanese young man.

"I suppose I do. They seem to me to be just about the same thing. I recognize that this is not true for a lot of people. For my best friend back home, for example."

The young composer said nothing for a while. Then he turned to his companion and erstwhile collaborator and spoke quietly in French.

"When one is visiting another continent," he would have said had he been speaking in English, "it is easy to think that one has fallen in love, and when one returns home, it would seem no great matter to speak about one's romantic and erotic adventures overseas. But I will not tell you about that part of my life in Paris."

"As romantic as that city is," said Bill.

"And the other."

Who's missing today?

Yes, *kabuki* with its peculiar costumes and stylized suicides that were already famous in the lurid newspapers. Fumiko

McCoy spent some afternoons remembering the non-famous suicides in her school and later at the Tokyo University of Foreign Studies. All the girls at school would mention sadness, shame, boredom, lost love or forbidden love, and how to finish with a jump or gas or the train. *Seppuku* was very romantic but it was reserved for men, and especially for men whose ancestors had been *samurai*.

Fumiko McCoy had always thought that if one of the girls in her class were going to kill herself it would have been Michiko. She was not famous, but her brother had been a famous child piano prodigy. Michiko was always talking about suicide. She had come back from her two years in Canada with a great sad wish in her eyes. Or she had begun to be sad soon after her return to Tokyo. She did not mention a suicide pact with a boyfriend. She never mentioned the name of her boyfriend, but everyone thought she had one. Maybe she had left one in Canada. She read books and magazine articles about suicide, and she attended the *kabuki*, always with a friend, but only because her family would not allow her to go alone.

But no, it was not Michiko who disappeared. Fumiko could not remember the name of her high school companion who had ceased to show up in class. She had not appeared in the newspapers and there was no ceremony for her departure. Sitting in her French classes with her best friend Michiko, she would let her mind drift. She would see the sadness in Michiko's eyes made more sad because of the new folds in her eyelids, and Fumiko would imagine stepping in front of a streetcar.

So when she met the tall white man with the big nose she thought of him as an alternative. She could choose death or life, and now it seemed that life was the same thing as this *hakujin* whom she first saw giving his arm to Michiko, to help her safely cross the street.

Did Fumiko steal this Bill McCoy from Michiko? She would never discuss this with Bill or with Michiko. For months they would be three young students visiting famous places in Tokyo, and gradually they would be a couple with their friend Michiko. No one said anything about it, but they all seemed to accept the changing pattern. It was kind of interesting because Bill was a friend of Michiko's brother the composer, but now he became more and more the boyfriend of Fumiko. The foreign boyfriend.

Fumiko imagined her boyfriend and herself holding hands and leaping from the new Tokyo Tower. She was not sad. It was just that she had always had a feeling deep inside her that she was going to be a suicide woman, maybe a famous suicide woman.

They had visited the tower with Michiko. When they got to the observation platform, Michiko stayed in the exact centre, where she could not see the huge city below her. Fumiko and Bill looked for a long time, as she pointed out the landmarks they could see from this unusual vantage. When they looked for her, Michiko was nowhere on the platform. They found her standing and smiling when they reached the ground.

"Did you know that the steel for this structure was reshaped from u.s. tanks that were damaged in the Korean War?" asked

Bill McCoy. He was always coming up with something like that.

Goaltending crisis?

Now Bill and Fumiko had received a letter from their son Frederick Akira McCoy, who was an exchange student at the University of Tokyo. "Did you know," he wrote, that if it is your birthday you get to go up to the observation tower free of charge, and you get a free piece of cake?"

"Kids today," said Bill McCoy. "They get the world handed to them on a bamboo platter."

But he fussed and worried about his only son all those thousands of kilometres away from home. Of course when . he had been there half a century earlier, you didn't make telephone calls back home because of the expense. You never thought that your parents might be worried about your living in the strange bombed land of earthquakes and suicides. You spent most of your time trying to differentiate yourself from the u.s. conquerors, trying, maybe, to be mistaken for a tall, bulb-nosed Japanese person.

At Bill's insistence, they did hear from Frederick on the telephone every Sunday, or as they called it in Japan, Monday. And thank goodness he was his father's son—they got letters from him about once a month.

"Did you know," he asked on the telephone, "that they now play ice hockey over here? *Hockey sur glace.* アイスホッケ — What a long way they have come since you were in Tokyo melding European and Nihonese serious music!"

"I had an extremely small and splintered part in Akira's beautiful piece," his father muttered. "And I don't know whether you can count ice hockey as coming a long way."

"Well, as you know, I am not exactly the star of my hockey team," said Frederick. "But as a Canadian here I was expected to play a role in defending the honour of the University of Tokyo ice hockey squad. So I played left wing on the third line."

"I suppose that's better than fattening up and throwing salt in a *sumo* ring," muttered the father.

"Until our goalie disappeared on us. Not exactly disappeared. He got drunk after we got beaten 11-0 by a high school team that had a few *gaijin* on it, and jumped off his parents' roof. He's still alive, but as things have turned out, I am now our goalie. If I get really good, I'm thinking of trying out for the Nippon Paper Cranes."

"Oh, Suckamacrychi!"

"Just joking, Dad."

Bill McCoy had no idea where his son's athletic skills had come from. His grandfather had been a fervent rugby player and boxer in Ireland before emigrating, but Bill McCoy the son, though he could swim and climb, never played on a team. His son Frederick had always played every sport that was made available, perhaps not in a starring role but with confidence.

"Oh, and Dad?" The question mark had travelled to an Earth satellite and back down. "I went to a performance of *Trois mouvements symphoniques*. It was terrific!"

What's important to you?

All summer long, on the other side of the country, the passenger jets land at Charlottetown Airport, and out their doors come all the Japanese girls. Many of them are wearing bright red woolen braids and carrying illustrated stories about Anne of Green Gables. They are going to take tour buses out along the oceanside highway to Green Gables Golf Course, where they will swarm the clubhouse, otherwise known as Green Gables farmhouse, forming queues to climb stairs and look into Anne's room with its little brass bed and flowery wallpaper.

Anne Shirley was or is a fictional person invented by Lucy Maud Montgomery, an Ontario woman who used to visit her cousins at their farm during her childhood summer vacations. Now all these Japanese girls have come around the globe to look at the place where Anne sleeps, and she's no fictional character. They have read her books at school and they have seen her adventures on television.

Little P.E.I. Anne of Green Gables was the first great Japanese *anime* hero. Beginning in 1979, the first series ran for fifty episodes. Millions of Japanese girls watched as their red-haired hero caught a cold, and because she lost her sense of taste, mistakenly used the wrong ingredient in a cake for Mrs. Allen. That was Episode 22. And Anne has never disappeared in Japan, as Heidi did. In 2009 a new series, *Before Green Gables*, was aired, and the planes kept coming to Prince Edward Island.

While these girls were watching the adventures of animated Anne in 1979, they were listening to its music by

Akira Miyoshi. So were the French girls who watched Anne—la maison aux pignons verts.

When a memorial DVD boxed set of the original series was released in 2008, a copy was delivered to Miyoshi *sensei*. We do not know whether he played any of the episodes on his flat screen television, but is it really so hard to imagine that he remembered the little Canadian girl and then revisited in his memory the young Canadian man he had spoken French with while walking under the ginkgo trees a half century ago?

Adele

It was still early but the café was jammed with people in overcoats so that the plate glass window in front was no longer transparent. All the tables and all the booths and the stools at the counter were full except the one table beside the front door, where the little old woman sat alone with her tea and some advertising brochures. She sat there every morning at this time, angrily studying the colourful offers of stoves and tires and television sets.

No one ever said good morning to her because it looked as if she could not hear any voice coming from the real world. She occasionally poured more water into her teacup, and angrily shoved a brochure to the bottom of the small pile in the middle of the table. Even on mornings when there were people standing outside waiting to get into the café, no one ever tried to sit at the table with her.

He was not used to being up so early, but this morning he had to go and talk to some kids in a nearby high school, so he was sitting with his buddy Willy and two strangers at a booth near the front. Lorna had just brought their cereal and boiled eggs and coffee, and Willy had already scooped two mouthfuls of Barley Blimps.

"Last week she threw rocks at the front window of a bus," Willy said.

"Why?"

"For her the bus represents the city. The city and the province and the country."

"She could be right," he said.

"Luckily, she could not throw hard enough to do any damage. Half the stones did not reach the windows, and the rest bounced off."

"What does she have against the city?"

"She has no money. It looks to her as if the city has lots and lots of money."

They had plenty of time before they had to get to Willy's school. They dawdled over their coffee while the people sharing their booth gathered up their overcoats and left. They were replaced by a young couple who knew enough not to bother trying to make conversation with the coffee drinkers. They must have been regulars at the café. Lorna the waitress poured refills absentmindedly. They looked at the old woman with her brochures.

"Her teabag is all used up," said Willy. "She's drinking warm water."

"What difference does it make to such an old body?"

"Tea might just be her only nourishment."

The old woman used her spoon to press down on the teabag. Lorna gave her a new one and some hot water.

"She's here every morning," said Willy. "I don't think I have ever arrived when she was not already here."

"Is there always such a crowd? Don't the waitresses need that table, or at least part of it?"

"Would you like to sit with her?"

"Does she keep them with her?"

"What? What are you talking about?"

"Her rocks. For throwing at the bus?"

The old woman was sitting perfectly straight. She had spilled a little milky tea into her saucer and now she was sipping from the saucer. If the place had not been so crowded with talking people, they would probably have heard her slurping the tea.

"It is as if they owe her something," he said. "It looks like an old story that goes a long way back."

"It always is," said Willy. "Isn't it?"

"Well, sometimes you are clear about the story."

"Clarity is subjective," said Willy.

"Did you make that up? That is a very deep paradox," he said.

"Thank you," said Willy.

They often talked to each other this way. They had been childhood friends and now Willy was a teacher in the east end. He was a bachelor. His friend thought that he was a lot smarter than most teachers, but probably that was a common thought among friends of teachers.

"When do we have to be there?"

"Don't worry. It's a five-minute walk. I haven't been late to school ever in my life," said Willy.

"I remember you in high school. What a suck you were."

"I was our class valedictorian."

"After all the effort I put into leading you astray."

"Your dad was a teacher. You had to act up," said Willy.

"They said I would wind up a nobody. Here I am forty years later sitting with you in an East End greasy spoon."

"What do you think she was like in school?"

"She was probably the most popular girl in her class. I hope so."

"Are you being sentimental or cynical?"

The old woman gathered her brochures into a neat pile. She pushed her cup and saucer up against the little metal pot. Then she stood up slowly and pushed her chair in. People were waiting to get her table. She picked up her brochures and her cheap old purse and walked slowly to the door. Four young people leapt at her table and sat down.

"Where does she go now?"

"You mean where is she going at the present time? Or where does she habitually go?" asked Willy.

He made a fist and held it in front of his old friend's nose.

"I have never followed her from the café because this is when I walk over to school."

"This means that you choose academic life over actual street life."

"No, I choose to put food on my table."

"So you have a table that is not in this café?"

They went outside and there was a light rainfall. He looked enquiringly at Willy, who replied by walking eastward, toward the school.

"It is true that I often eat dinner in that café," he said. "At night I don't really have time to cook because I have lessons to plan and tests to grade."

"You have never thought that you would rather be throwing stones at buses, I suppose."

"No, hombre, as you so often remind me, I am a lifetime school valedictorian. I don't carry stones."

They liked to drop Spanish words into their talk because they had taken Spanish together at university. When they were students they would spend whole days in Spanish.

"Did I piss you off a little there?"

They were under some trees now so the light rain did not reach them. Willy did not turn to him and smile, but he did not seem to be angry at him either.

"No. I am just getting into my schoolteacher mode."

"Is there anything I need to know about these kids?" he asked.

"*Nada. Nada y pues nada*," said Willy. Then he winked at his old friend.

Kassandra

Sometimes I tell myself that I should never have made eye contact with Kassandra Duncan. She was reading her poems to about twenty people in a basement room at the downtown library, and I was there in the line of duty. I did not sit in the front row, but I was up pretty close, because I didn't like to see any poet reading to just a few people in the back of the room.

I can't remember what she was reading, but knowing a little about her work I'd guess that it had something to do with being ironical about the vagaries of love and romance, especially in the physical area. Whatever was coming out of her mouth up there, it did not make anything like the impression I was getting from her eyes. I could have just let my glance shift away. I wouldn't have lost any points that way.

But I was a little stubborn, I guess. I kept looking at her eyes. The eyes I am talking about are partly brown and partly green, they are surrounded by greenish colour on her skin above and below them, and they are wide—not wide open, but wide. In all their width they were looking straight into my little brown eyes while her poems made their way to about forty ears, some of them attentive.

I have looked her poems up in the months since that reading. She could very well have been reading these lines:

> *He lay trapped in the*
> *turmoil of bed sheets around*
> *his ankles. She was painting his*
> *chest, candlelight mocking*
> *his efforts toward freedom.*
> *The window*
> *offered no breeze, the colour yellow*
> *was cold on his nipples*
> *and so on . . .*

And so on.

When the reading was over I caught her eye again, and just for fun I mouthed the words "How's about it?" Then she mouthed the words that I most like to hear from a woman: "Maybe later."

I think.

There followed weeks and months of normal life before it came about that I actually got somewhere with her. This time we were both attending a reading by another poet, an anti-academic guy I didn't much like. Kassandra and I were sitting in two hard chairs side by side, so I got to hear her whisper things toward the floor that suggested that she didn't much like the guy either.

"Why don't we," I said after we had escaped during the Q&A, "have a cocktail at the bar you get to when you walk up this set of stairs and out the north end of the library atrium?"

"I don't think it's an atrium," she said.

"I agree," I said. "I just can't think of the right word."

"You don't have to. You're not a poet."

Thank goodness I had no trouble putting up with this sort of thing, because before you could say Pee Wee Reese we were in the bar I had mentioned. I can't remember the name. In fact I can't remember ever seeing the name.

I think that it is around here that one is expected to say a few words in the way of description. She had long legs that were neither too thin nor too thick. They may have been slightly thick, but for me that has always made legs more desirable. It was late spring, so she was wearing a fairly short skirt and no stockings, just low tennis shoes with those tiny little white socks that are almost not there. Her knees were perfect, not really knobby but definitely the kind of bones you like to see. When she crossed her legs you got to see the shinbone and the smooth calf muscles behind it.

There's your description.

We had more than one cocktail each, but not enough to make us tell secrets and laugh too loud.

And then I was driving her home in my stupid old Chevy Biscayne. She pointed out a parking spot, so I began to get that familiar little rush of fear mixed with hope.

"Lock it," she said, not looking in my direction. "Not a perfect neighbourhood."

I could describe the neighbourhood or the outside of her building, but to tell the truth I wasn't looking at it much.

She took my hand and let it go while she dug into her bag for the key.

"I sort of feel as if I'm on a blind date," I said. It was not unusual for me to say stupid things when I got nervous.

"Just the opposite, actually."

Then she opened the door and before I knew it she opened another door, and there we were, in her place. There were three rooms, but one was a closet off the kitchen. One was the kitchen, where I sat at the table with a stemmed glass of cabernet franc in my hand. The third was going to have to be Kassandra's bedroom, I surmised.

"Bring your glass," she said, taking me by the other hand. In *her* other hand she had the bottle.

And led me into that room, which was larger than the other two put together. In the soft yellowish light I saw a bed with voluptuous piles of silk and other fabrics on it, a striped fainting couch, and a barber's chair with a little high table beside it. On this table she placed the wine bottle and my glass, which she refilled. Then she sat me upon the wine-coloured cushion of the barber's chair, and again before I knew it, a shiny pair of handcuffs had me attached to the scrollwork beneath the right armrest.

Then she left the room and closed the door. The wine was within reach of my left hand, so I drank some. This is going to be something, I heard myself say inside my head.

On the closed door there was an eye chart. I made it to the fourth row down, at which point all the letters looked like circles.

Then the door opened, and in she came. I pulled at my

handcuff. It would be a while till I calmed down enough to reach for my wine. First she stood still in the doorway, and the first thought I had was about her height. There was a lot of it. Then I pretty well stopped thinking altogether and just looked. She was extra tall because of the shoes. Very red. I thought that she must have been some sort of superhuman entity because no human could stand on heels that high and thin. Not without holding on to something. But then she began to walk on those heels, and every part of the front of her tall body was thrust forward. It became clear that she was going to walk closer to me, but she was going to walk from side to side, too.

Her shining blonde hair was piled high, with loose long curls descending here and there. Her wide eyes were definitely green, and her large mouth was partly open. There was a necklace of diamond-like stones wrapped tightly around her long neck. She was wearing a red something you might call a dress, except that it was more like a sock, just barely big enough to snug around her from the tops of her breasts to the tops of her knees. When she walked I was of the opinion that I may have been imagining the garment. The stockings on her long and just slightly thick legs must have been silk, there was such a sheen to them in the yellow light.

Now she stopped walking and just sort of quivered, right in front of me. You know what was happening to me inside my own garment. Not knowing what else to do with my semi-free hand, I used it to retrieve my glass of wine. I had to say something urbane.

"Whew!" I said. "Whew!"

She did not say a word. In fact she did not seem to make a sound, even on those heels. I tried to drink my wine without slurping. She wriggled out of her dress.

This was not an easy thing to do. I was in the classic male position of wanting her to hurry up and at the same time wanting her to take her time. Okay, I got to see that she was wearing a bra, a thing made mainly of lace and positioned principally on the underside of two achingly (you know what I mean) lovely orbs. Not those terrible big flesh balls made by surgery, but—oh, and then her skivvies came into view. I was so glad not to see a thong, that most off-putting garment in recent heterosexual history. Rather she sported those underpants that I always thought were French, the frilly ones that are loose around the tops of the legs, so you could slip a hand in there easily.

Before you could say "duh, uh, buh buh buh," she was standing in only these briefs, her stockings and her high heels, standing and then shifting her feet, almost dancing, and then moving just the slightest bit, with the front of her silken garment an inch from my face, an inch because that was as far forward as I could lean.

Then that panty was, because of a graceful gesture involving a few of her long fingers, off. And so, you might say, was I.

"Phew!" I said.

What an attractive smile then passed over her lips, as she handed me a little key and pointed toward the door. By the time I had freed myself from the handcuffs, she had snuggled into her fluffy bed. I took a step toward her, but she again pointed at the door.

"Make sure the outside door is locked when you go," she said.

"Can I see you again?" I asked.

"I am not so sure that is the right verb," she said, and turned her shoulder away.

2.

Maybe I should have quit going to poetry readings. For sure, I should have known that she would be attending Nicole Brossard's reading at the Born Yesterday Gallery. After the reading and the question period, I was doing my usual thing—waiting till the twittering crowd around the poet had thinned out before going over and administering an old-time brotherly hug to indicate silently that this person and I go back a long way.

Of course Kassandra Duncan was doing something similar, and I guess that it was inevitable that we would wind up giving each other a hug. I suppose that would have been all right, and I could then have walked out into the drizzle that had been making its presence known on the big window-pane. It sounded as if it might be turning into sleet. My Biscayne was a block away, but I had the key in my hand.

"Can I cadge a ride home?" Guess who.

"Sure."

Drive drive drive drive.

"Want to come in for a drink?"

"What do you have?"

"I have what you want," she said, and by then we were at

the door. I made a big show of shaking rain off my raincoat in the hallway, and then I toed off my Merrells in such a way as to suggest that my purpose was to protect her floor and so on.

But before you could say Nérée Beauchemin, I was back in the barber's chair, this time with a whisky and soda by my left hand, and my right wrist secured as before. There was one more difference. I was wearing a very efficient blindfold. From the scent it gave off, I thought that it might also serve sometimes as my captor's apparel.

There was no radio, no music in this room or the next. In fact, all I could hear was the blood pulsing in my left temple, and a little tinnitus in my right ear. I was going to reach carefully for my drink, but I decided to keep completely quiet, let her make the first move.

I thought I heard the door to the kitchen open, a short squeak. Then nothing. Then something.

"What?" I whispered.

"Shhh," said the darkness, or someone in it. I sat very still, my back just a wee bit arched. I actually cocked my ear, or rather tilted my head a little.

I heard a zipper being zipped, or, I hoped, unzipped. I tried to picture what she had been wearing at the reading. A short skirt in a houndstooth pattern, and nylon stockings, or probably pantyhose. I heard the skirt land on the floor. I was listening harder than I had ever listened in my life.

I heard a nylon stocking rub against another nylon stocking, one of the top five sounds in the world.

Then near to my right ear—a mouth inhaling air. I made a hopeless move with my right hand, till it stopped hard, like a dog at the end of its leash. Then the mouth exhaled, with a light groan. I wanted to ask for a number of things, but I wanted to hear where this was going, so I kept my mouth shut. I felt like groaning myself, what with the turmoil in my garment.

I was not sure about what I was hearing next, but I wanted it to be the sound of a shirt being undone and dropped to the floor, followed by the unhooking and dropping of a bra. But soon some human sounds became identifiable. Close to me, straight in front of my face, the sounds a mouth can make, an air kiss, some wetness breathed in and out, air that sounded warm. I heard skin on skin. I heard a faint groan from deep inside somewhere. A breathy laughter almost inaudible.

This sort of thing went on, and there were pauses that always seemed too long. I lifted my whisky and drank as quietly as I could. Each time a pause came I thought it might be the last long one.

I never did finish my drink. There came a little clinking sound, and then I was aware that my right wrist was being released.

"Now go. Find your own way out. You know," came her quiet breath.

"Can I take off my blindfold?"

"Outside. Go."

3.

I took Kassandra Duncan's black silk scarf to every reading I went to for the next few months, but she did not show up until early in the new year, at a launch for George Stanley's new book *The On Deck Circle*.

"I was hoping to hear from you," I whispered in her ear.

"You never get the verb right," she said, then sat straight in her wooden chair and attended to the poems.

A lot of people telling a story like this would stop here to describe the poet and maybe offer a few lines from his reading that night. But look, if you want that sort of thing, why don't you just go and have a look at one of the poems from the above-mentioned collection? You'll be doing yourself a favour. George Stanley was on record, maybe a year earlier, as saying that he would never write any short poems again, that if anything he would perhaps offer a second volume to his last book-length poem. But *The On Deck Circle* is a terrific collection, and by the time that he got to the second poem, I had almost forgotten about the blonde poet who was sitting beside me, with a black silk scarf wrapped around her hands.

But all good things come to an end, and all bad things have to start sometime, and you will be pleased or disgusted, depending on your own standards of post-poetical behaviour, to hear that I gave Kassandra a ride home. In fact I had even waited around while she got in line to have her copy of the book signed.

"Wine or something else?" she asked, while putting her bag on the kitchen table.

What verb, I was wondering, and what drink should go with what verb? I thought I might stump her.

"How about a Fernet-Branca?"

"Would you accept a Jägermeister?"

To tell the truth, I couldn't tell the difference. They both taste like a combination of medicinal herbs and cleaning agents, and even their labels are similar. I accepted a Jäger-meister. When the small wet glass was in my hand, I went into the other room and climbed up onto the barber's chair. For a couple of minutes I sat and sniffed the aromatic liquid and sipped at it and heard a poem in my head. I think that it started off as a George Stanley poem and slowly turned into a Kassandra Duncan poem.

> *My uncles washing dishes while the aunts*
> *chased after one another with open clothes pins,*
> *who left the taps running, I asked, and who*
> *will put us kids to bed?*

was the way it ended or didn't end.

Because then Kassandra entered the room, closing the door behind her. She wore a frilly white cotton shift that descended to her bare ankles, and she was holding both the Jägermeister bottle and the black silk scarf. This latter she held in one hand, while in the other she took the one of my hands that was not holding a beverage and led me to the bed I had on more than one occasion fancied reclining upon. She bade me then to hoink myself up against the headboard so that I was almost lying down but still able to handle my herbal drink. Then she fixed the black silk scarf around my head so that I was without sight. At least my hands were free now.

"If you promise not to reach for anything," she whispered, "I will leave you unfettered."

"I think that when you say fettered or unfettered, you're talking about feet," I said.

"No need to be so strict," she whispered, a little farther away now, I calculated.

"I suggest unrestrained," I said.

"Shh," she advised.

I reached carefully to set my glass on the bedside table. Then I did some thinking, not intellectual thought, but this sort of thing: okay, we seem to have had something to look at, and then something to listen to. So now here I am again with the black silk item over my eyes. What will it be this time?

Lemon. I smelled a freshly cut or shaved lemon. It was not lemon-scented polish or cake or soap. It was the real item. Maybe my favourite scent in the world, probably many other people's too.

"Mmm," was my unstudied response.

I could not hear bare feet, but I reasoned inwardly that this was not a hearing experience. I tried to hear bare feet, though. The name Descartes zipped through my cranium, then disappeared. But really, the experience was not that cerebral. I smelled a brand-new clothbound book.

"Let me sniff it," I said.

My nose actually nearly touched the paper where verso met recto.

"Viking," I guessed.

"Close," she said. "Random House."

I was going to make a smart remark about knowing the author, but I felt something push the mattress down a little near me. It could have been a knee, I thought.

Once again there was a woman's mouth near mine, but no faint groan this time, just a smooth exhalation of breath.

"Gin," I said, confidently. "Maybe Bombay."

"Ballantine."

Another depression of the mattress. Now there was something near my face. The scent was some kind of shampoo I would never buy because of the expense, but I do think there was an intimation of cedar. Many are the times that I would stand with my nose against a tree, a silly thing to do, but a lifetime requires such occasions, don't you think?

There followed a series of subtle commotions on the mattress, and I was permitted the slight odour of toes, a whiff of evening armpit, oh yes, and right after she said, "Be very still," the unmistakable attar of quim.

I tried not to sniff loudly, not wanting to appear crude, but I stayed perfectly still, all but one part of me, of course, and drew breath deeply. Till she was gone and the mattress reacquired its former shape.

"Count to ten and remove your scarf," she said. "Then you can find your way out."

"When will I see you—"

But by then I knew that no amount of synesthesia would get me where I wanted to go. So I headed out and down the stairs again.

4.

Of course, you know what happened. This time it was a reading by David McFadden, who was making one of his rare visits to the coast. There is no poet in the country easier to listen to than David McFadden, because he combines talent and accomplishment with sentiment and surprise, and I do not know what more to ask for unless you are talking free beer.

There I was. There she was. There we went. Why bother with trying to remember the details of the car ride and the door opening?

By this time I had figured out what she was doing, her artistry with the five senses. Seeing and hearing and smelling were taken care of. As I kicked my Merrells into the corner of her kitchen I wondered which we would be trying out this evening, and I have to tell you that I was looking forward. There would be no more resistance or delaying humour from me. If there were going to be handcuffs or blindfolds or any other kind of constraints, bring them on! Rope, shackles, nose plugs, whipped cream, what the hell!

Okay, whipped cream is not a constraint, but I did not rule it out once it had sprung to mind.

It turned out to be the blindfold, but not with a black scarf this time. This time I was supplied with a mask that covered my whole face except for three breathing holes. I was seated in a simple wooden chair and before I could say Spider Robinson, the visible world went away. I don't know what the mask looked like from the outside, but from the inside I was in utter blackness. I sat up straight with my back barely touching the chair's back.

I heard high heels walking away from me, and then before I could hear anything else I felt a hand on my shoulder.

"You will notice that your hands are neither handcuffed nor tied," she said. "Your instructions are that you must remain seated and that you may not use anything but your hands in this game of touch."

This one was the hardest to endure. What a combination of gratification and frustration. No, it was neither of those two. Can you be delirious and come to your senses at the same time, I wondered. The poet Robert Kroetsch had it right when he said you want to get there, where you are going, but you want the journey never to stop. He said that is what writing a long poem is about. Well, I am no poet, but as I was sitting in Kassandra's room with a mask over my face, I knew what he meant.

Kassandra stood next to me and turned while I gently palmed her torso. What global skin I felt, what roundness and what ovals, what nipples sticking out and what moistness where the heat was. I am not going to try to describe her invisible but lovably resistant and giving body. My hands knew more than my eyes had ever seen. For a moment Kassandra stood right in front of my seated body, and her feet must have been as far apart as her shoulders were. I felt her. Then I tried to get more comfortable.

"You are not allowed to do that," she said.

"It's just that my pants are too tight. I can't bear it," I said.

"No, you don't touch yourself, only me."

"You can touch me," I suggested.

She laughed a little, breathing while she did so.

"Please," I said, and inside my head I heard myself saying the word many times. "Please, I would like to follow the urgings of nature, and I think I believe that you must feel them too, somewhat."

She squatted beside me so that I could feel her shoulders, the back of her neck. Please, I said inside my head.

"Do you remember the first time we talked, you and I?"

"Uh, uh, uh." That's all I could manage to say.

"It was three years ago, in the taproom of the Arrow Hotel after a poetry reading. I could tell you who had been reading and even the titles of some of her poems, but you wouldn't be interested. What you wanted to know, in your Pale Ale way, was my middle name."

"I always want to know middle names," I said.

"After some creative, ah, urging on your part, I told you mine."

"I don't remember," I said, and my hands were unmoving on her splendid ass.

"When you remember," she said, and she was walking away, "I will give serious consideration to the urgings of nature."

The usual: mask, doorway, stairs, drive home. That's where the urgings of nature took over for the time being.

5.

Now I know that you have been checking off the five senses, and as this is a realist story, you know that there will be no fooling around with the so-called sixth sense. You also know that whatever happens will happen after a poetry reading. Right. This time it was a reading by Sharon Thesen. If you have not been to a reading by Sharon Thesen, do yourself a favour—travel to wherever she is scheduled to give a reading and plunk yourself in the best chair early.

When she wrinkles her nose and mentions damson plums, you can taste the plums. If one of her lyric poems has strawberry ice cream in it, you might want to carry a spoon.

I tried to talk with Kassandra about Thesen's poems on the way to her place, but she apparently doesn't like Thesen's work.

"You're saying it's a matter of taste?" I asked, not altogether innocently.

"I could just get out here and walk home," she said.

"No, no, it's raining cats and dogs,"

"Sprinkling, perhaps."

"It's raining kittens and puppies."

"Don't be cute. You're not on Facebook now."

As you can see, I was trying to get myself in a spot where I could be the mover of events. I didn't want her to get the idea that I was just her plaything. Sure, she had published four books of poetry, but I had reviewed forty, though none of hers.

I had looked up her name, though. Κασσανδρα. Her parents were Greek immigrants, and sometimes there were Greek phrases in her poems, as if we were back in the days of Ezra Pound and his bunch. I had also tried to look up her middle name, but though she was all over the Internet, her middle name was a cybersecret.

I let her off at her door and went to find a parking spot. This meant a two-block walk in the light rain back to her place, and a one-minute wait at the door before she buzzed me in.

She let me in and wordlessly gestured toward the bedroom. A few minutes later she came into that room, saw me sitting on the maroon barber's chair, and motioned me toward the bed. I kicked off my Merrells and sat up with my back against the headboard. The reason I did this was twofold. I did not want to appear boorishly eager, and I wanted a position from which I could better look at her. I say this because of her costume.

Or lack of costume, I should say. She was wearing three items: a wide mauve ribbon in her hair, a pair of high-heeled slippers, silver in colour, and a white gossamer item that fell like a robe but was almost transparent and would have been no protection against any cold air I have ever felt. In her left hand she held a little porcelain bowl, and in her right hand a teaspoon. She leaned forward, thus creating a stupefied expression on my face, I am sure, and put a spoonful of something into my quite-moist mouth.

It took a moment to register.

Jelly. Black elderberry.

I smiled my appreciation. She reached behind her some-where and came back with something that looked like a small cookie. When she gently placed it in my mouth, I bit off half and let it rest on my tongue. Then I chewed it very slowly.

"Hibiscus," I said. "Better in tea."

She now had a small jar in her left hand. Into this she poked her right forefinger after having moistened it in her lovely mouth. That's when I noticed the dark red colour on her generous mouth. She inserted her finger between my more ordinary lips.

This one took me quite a long time.

"Argan oil," I said. "At first I thought it was hazelnut oil, but there is a little *soupçon* of a darker, shall we say, bitterness at the end."

"Mmm. You are very good," she murmured. "Better than I would have thought. This may be your primary sense. That interests me."

"Thank you. May I remove my shirt?"

"I will put away these culinary items while you remove whatever you want."

Naturally, I took off just about everything. My excitement was beginning to show. I will try to be as delicate in narrative now as I was that hour.

When she got back I was virtually without clothing, or so I thought.

"Take those black socks off or go home," she advised.

They were off in a trice, and I don't think I ever saw them again. Now here she was, her gossamer wrap or whatever open in front. I started to make a move, but she put her hand on my arm, signifying that she was going to do whatever moving there would be for now. Her fingers signified again, and the back of my head was on a big fluffy pillow.

She placed two fingers in my mouth, and I knew that she had cut into the skin of a lemon again. Her generous lips were on my mouth, and stayed there while they seemed to pulse. I tasted an unanticipated blend of raspberry and coconut. Her tongue had been near curry recently. I did not know where this fifth sense would take me, nor how far, but it was everything I could do not to cup her breast or buttock with my hand, something she used her strong fingers to remind me not to attempt. There was nothing I could do about the growth of my wand, but she did no suggesting thereabouts.

She placed a breast on my face, and I received the scent of her skin, partly natural, partly the result of exotic emollients such as Mayan or Inca princesses used to keep themselves sweet beneath the sun. If you have been around, you know that everybody has their own scent. No one's skin, as far as I knew, smelled like Kassandra's. Naturally, I tasted it. Her long nipple was in my mouth, then my tongue ran around the bottom of her breast, then up her side and into her armpit. A surprise had been waiting for me there, the divine flavour of mock orange blossoms.

Kassandra was like a soft muscular python as she coiled about me. She offered all the countries of her planet. I had never felt so sensitive in my life. I put my hands behind me, under me, defining my world with my mouth. When I heard a slipper land on the floor I knew what was coming. I licked all along the sole of her foot. I put my tongue between her toes, all of them, wondering at the perfect mixture of toe jam and hyacinth.

Or a gentle but firm anaconda, now she was astride the bottom part of my ribcage, a knee beside me, another on the other side. I heard what sounded like private laughter, quiet above me, as if she had finally allowed it to escape her throat. Now she yanked the pillow from below my head and put a hand on the bed sheet beside each of my ears. She did this in order to hoist herself nimbly to where she wanted to be, and now I can tell you that that's where I wanted her to be. She was grasping the top of the headboard with her strong hands, and the top half of her body was resting on my welcoming mouth.

I tasted and tasted—such was her intent—while she very slowly set herself moving. I tasted something faintly familiar though I had never tasted Kassandra before. My eagerness to recall what it was I was tasting caused me to please the woman above me, I was given by her whispered exclamations to understand. Yes, there was a flavour most female, sister perhaps to your own, but there was something else, something that appeared, then disappeared, then returned, teasing my imagination, if you can be said to have an imagined flavour.

I wanted, of course, to search my mind to find it, but I was having such a good time, and the woman above me was apparently so delighted, that any memory I was going to have would have to be involuntary, a flash.

Lorraine. No, not a woman's name, but the region of northeastern France, nearly Luxembourg. More precisely, the commune of Commercy. I was there twenty years before, a poor lonely young man behind a rain-streaked window, spending some of his few remaining francs at Patisserie Richy.

Where I bit at last into a lemony and almondy sponge cake shaped liked a seashell.

"Madeleine!"

I think that my expostulation was muted, as if I had a mouth full of a French confection. I pulled my face free for a moment.

"Your middle name is Madeleine!" I said, with a bit of triumph in my voice.

"You don't have to decide so soon," she said. "Give it time."

But now memories inundated my mind. A bead of perspiration fell from her breast onto my forehead.

"Madeleine! You told me. You were wearing glasses that day. Glasses with blue rims, the kind of blue I remember from our kitchen curtains when I was about ten."

Kassandra kept moving, so that part of the time my words were probably somewhat obscured. Part of the time she focused her attention on my chin. I have, if I say so myself, a good chin.

"We were not in the taproom of the Arrow Hotel. We were in the Bean Around the World coffee shop in the 4400 block of West Tenth, which enterprise is mentioned in Spider Robinson's book *Callahan's Key*. We were sitting at the counter that runs along the sidewalk window, and you were letting me read your newest poem in your handwriting. The poem was called 'Peculiar Trains.' It started like this:

> *My grandmother, who was also Bulgarian*
> *and wore the apron for it, said she descended*
> *from kestrels and the sky*
> *so don't you bring home any carved wooden boys*
> *she warned me, or I will stretch you*
> *in a poplar tree, the noisiest home in the forest.*

The poem was three pages long in your raptor handwriting. I can remember every word, every bit of punctuation."

"Ah. Ah," she said.

"You were strikingly beautiful that day with the light from

an unusually blue sky finding you inside that big north-look-ing window. You were wearing two-tone leather boots and a short tweed skirt with a bit of bare thigh, all of a bare knee and a bit of bare calf showing. Just like those Claes Olden-burg knees from 1966 that were cast in flexible latex and coated in polyurethane, if I remember rightly."

"Ah," she said, working on my chest now. Perspiration fell on my face. I was remembering everything about that day in the Bean.

"Only one of the tables behind us was in use. There were two little old ladies sitting there, both of them, oddly, wear-ing knitted tams, one powder blue, one ecru. From what I could hear they were discussing a 1954 movie titled *Ele-phant Walk*. They were agreed that it starred Elizabeth Tay-lor, and that it had Peter Finch in it, but they could not agree on the male lead. The one in powder blue insisted that it was William Holden, and the one in ecru said she didn't think so. Well, I didn't say anything to them, but the answer was Dana Andrews."

"Shut," she said between short breaths.

"A strange request, given the circumstances, Madeleine."

"Up," she said.

"Good idea," I said.

"You have earned the opportunity to fully obey the urg-ings of nature," she said, sliding down my body.

"You just split an infinitive," I said.

"That will prove to be the least of your worries," she told me.

Barbara

I found my father in the heart wing on the eighth floor of Toronto General Hospital.

"Oh, I know it very well, believe me! You don't have to tell me about that place. I wish to God I never heard of it! Let me tell you, if they try to put me in that place I will raise such a stink like you never heard."

Or smelled, perhaps? Stink?

"Smelled? It was terrible! I said to Maury when I finally got home, I am never going back to that hellhole unless I have a gas mask on my face. It was like the old dump up Choate Road, you remember that? How did you ever talk me into going up there with your funny friends?"

He had wires taped to his chest.

"Who? Oh, your father! Oh, my god, wires? I think they use those to zap electricity into a person's heart. I always thought your father was a barrel-chested man, a lumberjack sort of fellow. It just goes to show."

What?

"You never can tell."

My father did not seem to mind.

"Let me tell you, Verna, your father is a saint! If it was Maury in there with wires all over his body? He would be complaining all up and down the hospital. He would have his secretary, that dowdy woman, doesn't know how to apply lipstick, he would have her telephoning the premier's office. He's a combination of pussy and loudmouth, that Maury. You know, I love him, but he is not an easy man to live with."

I had to wait for an hour in the emergency waiting room.

"If you ask me, that's terrible. Verna, I would hate to add up all the taxes we have paid in the last ten years, and you know how much of that went to OHIP? It seems like the more we pay, the longer the waits are. I know a woman, neighbour of ours, had to wait three hours in emergency to get her lungs listened to. She was coughing and horking all that time, probably infected ten other people in that waiting room. Can you imagine?"

I went to see my father. He was sitting up in bed in a curtained-off corridor.

"Like every time we come home from somewhere. In the waiting room and in the plane, there's people coughing all around me. How many of them cough into the inside of their elbow? Are you kidding me? People just don't care about other people any more. When I was a kid people carried hankies and coughed into their hankies, just like in the Health Canada posters. Remember them?"

I was not surprised by the doctor's news.

"Doctors! At least you don't see them smoking so much any more. I remember my gynecologist. Doctor Export Plain, I always called him. Used to have a green pack of ciggies right there on his desk. He wasn't a cougher, I have to say that. But come on, it's not as if we're just now finding out about cigarettes being bad for you. I know you never smoked, Verna, but I started smoking when I was fourteen, and quitting smoking was the hardest thing I ever did. Well, except when Treeny was born."

When I saw from my father's face that he felt it—

"Verna, you are so lucky you never had to go through childbirth. They say there is no pain like it in the world, and I believe them. It took a day and a half for Treeny to get born, and just about the same for Kyle. I can tell you I hated everyone, hated the doctor and all the nurses, and those little shits who were trying to get out or trying to stay in, I don't know which. Hated everyone in the hospital, and Maury for getting me pregnant in the first place. It's a good thing he was too chicken to be there in the delivery room or I would have told him how much I hated him. I would have said the worst words I know, and I would have said them pretty damned loud. As it was I said things pretty loud anyway. I called the obstetrician a cocksucker, did I ever tell you that?"

Maybe once or twice.

"He didn't bat an eyelash, just kept sitting there with his hands in me up to the elbows, it looked like. They have a mirror up there, you know, so you can see what's going on, like you want to, eh? All I remember seeing in the mirror was the bald spot on the back of Dr. Grabby's head."

The next day he was himself again.

"Maury said we ought to try having the baby at home. Latest thing, he said. Up yours is what I said. I was born in the hospital. My mother was born in the hospital. All my friends and all my relatives were born in the hospital, I said. That's what the hospital is for, starting babies on their way. Hospitals are all about the beginning of life. Skiing accidents and childbirth."

"Now why would I want to get myself operated on?" said my father reasonably.

"Operations! Don't get me started on operations!"

"Think of the risk at my age, and—"

"I've had more operations than you can shake a stick at. Started as a little girl, the usual tonsils and adenoids, elementary school. Appendix, high school. Did you know they have never found any use for the appendix? That's what I heard. But does that stop the damned thing, whatever it is, from going bad? I was in hospital for a week that time, and could hardly walk after I got out. Okay, I guess everyone gets those, tonsils and appendix. But when I broke my hand punching a cement wall instead of Maury, they fixed it in an operating room, I remember the bright light overhead, slept in that room for a while after all. That counts as an operation, eh? Fixing my hand. Had it in a plaster cast for two months."

"—what for? A few years at the outside."

"Gall bladder. Maybe they know what a gall bladder is for, but I sure as hell don't. You know what a gall bladder is for? If it's for something, how come they could take mine out and

I can get by without it? But let me tell you, I couldn't lift anything for a long time after they took out that little sucker. Maury, for the first time in his life he has to lift something, the poor guy. My heart bleeds for him, you should pardon the expression."

"I think the best thing for me—"

"Hey, you remember that song from when we were kids? *My heart yearns for you, burns for you, something something for you . . .* "

This is what I would have expected of him. Are you listening at all?

"Please come back to me. If you're in Oklahoma, I'll follow you. If you're in Arizona, I'll be there too. Something like that. *Hmm hmm, hmm hmm hmm hmm hmm.*"

Judith, my younger daughter, whom you seem to have forgotten about, came to meet me at Toronto Airport two days ago.

"Oh, I remember Judith. Wouldn't let anyone call her Judy. That's the way it is these days. No one is Mike any more; they're all Michael. Thank god Treeny and Kyle are just Treeny and Kyle. I think it started with those Negro athletes, and you have to call them African-Americans nowadays, I've heard. When we were kids, those Negro athletes were called Willy and Jackie. Now it's all Michael and Anthony and so on. Except all the ones that are called La Keeshan and Shakeer-Zann. You should hear what Maury calls them, but then maybe you shouldn't."

No, I shouldn't, I guess. Anyway, Judith said she did not know where her sister Nichola was, exactly.

"Isn't that the way with kids now, eh? We shouldn't worry about them so much, is what I say. When Kyle got into that trouble with the drugs and all, and it wasn't his fault, he was just driving the car, I thought how have I failed as a parent? I talked to them till I was glue in the face. I warned them about who they were associating with. They wouldn't listen. They never listen. I talk to them and talk to them, but—"

Blue. Blue in the face.

"Exactly. If people don't listen once in a while, where are we going to end up? You're lucky you just had one child, Verna. God, I don't know how often I've phoned the hospital in the middle of the night, hoping my kids weren't there. You're lucky you don't have to be calling the hospital all the time. What's Judy doing these days? Is she married?"

She brought the boy she is living with, whose name is Don. They were driving to Mexico in the morning.

"Mexico! Now that's a dangerous place from all I've heard. I'm a little younger than you, but I can still remember when it was all guitars and trumpets and hot food and *mañana*. Mexico and Argentina and all those *mañana* places. Means later, I'll do it later, time right now for a little fiesta. Nowadays it's all drug cartels and dead bodies in the street. I would just about crap if my kids went to one of those places."

Judith said she didn't know where my other daughter Nichola was, exactly. She said Nichola had moved out of her apartment (that dump).

"Ah, my sainted aunt Tillie, I know how hard it is to find a decent apartment in Toronto these days. It's probably a lot easier in Calgary, where you live."

Vancouver.

"Partly it's the real estate agents, and partly it's the rich im-migrants. You probably have the same problem in Calgary. Those agents, all that fake blonde hair hanging over their shoulders, those spike heels. You don't have to tell me what's going on. If they weren't trying to sell houses I wonder what they would be doing, eh? And those rich immigrants, well, you know where they're from. Wasn't too long ago they were walk-ing around behind water buffaloes, now they drive around in fancy foreign cars and have season's tickets to see the Raptors. You know what I'm talking about. Maury and I worked our asses off for forty years and we still owe some on our first mort-gage. But these people? They buy houses without seeing them, and then they knock them down and build bigger houses. Got a four-car garage instead of a water buffalo."

Once, when my children were little, my father said to me, "You know those years you were growing up—well, that's all just a kind of blur to me."

"Hah! Isn't that just like a man? A blur. Maybe women are just more likely to notice things in the first place and more likely to remember them in the second place. I don't think there has been one day in my life I don't remember like it was yesterday. Do you remember the day your Judy came over to my place and got her head stuck in the chimney flue?"

Nichola.

"It was no joke. We had to call the fire hall and go next door and borrow a pail of margarine. Geeze, I wonder if I ever paid Sally back? Boy, that kid of yours could sure make a racket! How long did it take you to get all that margarine out of her hair? You remember Sally, don't you? Sally Riis, pronounced it Reese, like the hockey player, Pee Wee Reese."

Base—

"Played for the Maple Leafs back when they were good. Used to win the Stanley Cup all the time. Not like nowadays, they never make the playoffs but they don't care, they always sell out every game, and you see bozos driving all over Ontario with Maple Leafs flags flying out of their cars. But I have to say this, you don't see those rich immigrants flying Maple Leafs flags out of their expensive imported cars. Drive the cars your neighbours build, that's what I say. Maury and me? We've had nothing but GM cars all the time we were married. Had an Austin once, back in the sixties, and that car gave us more grief than gravy if you know what I'm saying. I don't even know the names of the expensive cars those rich immigrants drive up and down the street, looking for houses to buy."

So it turns out that my father has been having sex with one of the young men who deliver breakfast. Young fellow drives an Elantra, apparently.

"I look at the pictures in the real estate people's window on Bloor, not that I'm interested in moving, you know, but just to look at the prices, see what our old place is worth now. It makes you sick, is what it does. What if you were a young couple and your husband just got transferred here from, say, Sault-Ste-Marie? How in the dickens would you ever be able to afford a house, much less an apartment."

I have been reading Dickens again. He seems totally dif-

ferent when you come back after all these years. Have you
ever read *Barnaby Rudge*? It's a Dickens I had never encountered before.

"What? It's hard to get used to, if you ask me. When we
were younger we always heard about those poor starving
children in Asia. Eat your supper, our parents would say,
think about all those hungry children in Asia. Now they
seem to be the only people who can afford Toronto real estate, or Calgary, I imagine. Now those children in Asia are
grown up and buying our real estate out from under us. And
from what I heard they don't even live here. They're all back
home in China and India and Argentina."

Started with a little finger stuff, this Asian boy delivers
breakfast to my father and slips his hand under the covers.
Boy from Argentina, I understand, speaks with a Chinese
accent.

"See? What did I tell you? Take all the jobs away from
Canadians, too. I've got relatives, went all the way through
school, can't get a decent job. Think the union's going to
help them? All the union bosses have names you can't pro-
nounce. There was a time a young man or woman could
finish up school and step right into the labour force, lots
of opportunities just out there waiting. The mayor's right—
all those pointy-head sociologists living in downtown
condos and drinking immigrant coffee at five bucks a shot,
they need a dose of real life. The mayor's the friend of the
ordinary guy, he'll talk to you on the phone. Doesn't give a
shit, pardon the French, for all those big words and little
pointy heads."

Is there anything I can say to you that will result in the beginning of a conversation?

"Bunch of Einsteins sitting around drinking fancy coffee, don't have a clue what is going on in real life."

What do *you* think E equals, Barbara?

"I was never any good at math, is that what you're talking about?"

I'm trying to tell you about my father and his grandchildren.

"Remember how they used to tell us we'd need math in our future lives? All these years I have never had to use math once. There's a calculator on my phone if I need it. Have you ever used algebra in your life? Remember we always called it 'algae bra'? Now, you take your regular bra. I've made a lot of good use out of a lot of those. You were a B-cup, weren't you? You are so lucky, believe me. Maury always used to compliment me on what he called my 'rack,' and I always wondered, what's the connection with a buck deer with a good rack. Never got that one. But you know, I always see him checking out the chests of those skinny girls."

You had just about the biggest gazongas in high school, I remember that, Barbara. I also remember how you used to accidentally touch boys with them.

"Maury always made sure I knew how he felt about them. He used to sink his chin in his neck and say, 'By Jove,' he would say, 'there's two moons in the sky tonight.' Still does from time to time, though I have to say the sky isn't where you'll see them. Ha ha."

And by Jove, we'd as likely as not see four of them.

"Oh, Verna, still the same old joker I always knew. Well, I have to get going. Look at the time. I was supposed to be at the wellness centre ten minutes ago. Say hi to your family for me. I hope they're all doing okay. Didn't you have a little boy with some health issues?"

Little Ganymede, yes. He's been dead for ten years.

"Okay, give them all my best wishes, hafta scoot."

Ichiko

Like me, you have probably wondered how you would handle things if you won a big lottery. That's what the paper always wants to know. Everybody loved the guy in the fishing village on the coast up north who won $20 million and just started spending it on the folks in his little town. Said he figured he didn't have a lot of time to live, and whatever relatives he had down south had never shown any interest in him up till now. He didn't wait for outfits in his town to come after him, either. He went to the local home-improvement guy and paid him top dollar to replaster and paint the town library. Then he bought the home-improvement guy a new truck. The nice thing about the story is that people didn't come from out of town to try to pry the dollars away from him. He had let them know that if any of the money was going to go out of town, it was going to get there by way of people who lived there.

The most common story is that some guy says he is going

to pay off all the mortgages in his family and maybe get himself a new truck. Or else it's six women all work in the same office, and they are going to head for Baja California. Sometimes you hear about a winner who is broke and addicted two years later. A lot of the time you don't hear who won. You know it's some guy or woman is consulting lawyers and estate planners and psychologists and so on. They have a whole industry going, organizing the lives of lucky ticket holders.

I am not a lottery winner. I bought maybe two lottery tickets in my life, and that was years ago when that business was just starting. I am old enough to remember when lotteries just happened in third-world countries, where immorality gave way to economic hardship. When I was a girl, buying lottery tickets was illegal, along with taking drugs and pornography.

No, but I did come into a lot of money all at once and unexpectedly. Maybe right here I should introduce myself. My name is Ichiko Benitez. I may be the only person in the country with that name. I am not exactly sure how I got that moniker, because I was born here. If I had known my parents when I was growing up, I might be able to tell you all about it. But they died before they even got their citizenship papers, and of course I was an only child. That's what some official told me before disappearing forever from my life.

I have done some reading, and I learned that a lot of people in mixed marriages give the kid a first name that belongs to the mother's family or at least nationality. Makes sense. I think that Ichiko means first daughter in Japanese. My middle name is Jimena. Before he left my life forever, some very white government guy told me that my parents were from Dominica. Of course I checked that out. There are seventy thousand people living in Dominica, and most of them are African by background. The rest are British or French, mainly. No one in Dominica speaks Spanish or Japanese.

I long-ago guessed that the dolt with the government job had not been told Dominica, but rather the Dominican Republic, a country in which almost everyone speaks Spanish. My guess was confirmed for me on the day when I was told I had become rich. I was further told that if I had bothered to keep a record of my family I might have become rich several years earlier. It had taken lawyers and civil servants, even though they were much better informed than the person mentioned above, a time of Dickensian proportions to find out that Ichiko Benitez was the only living descendent of Oscar Santiago Benitez y Ojoa.

I know that you have the sense not to ask how much my stunning inheritance amounted to, nor how my grandfather had accumulated that sum on an island whose two countries are not famous for their high standard of living. Even if there had been someone to ask, I would not have asked. Anyway, I was pretty well used to living a modest lifestyle, so I was in no hurry to start looking for Swiss watches and German cars. I just signed whatever people wanted me to sign whenever they got around to sticking the paper in front of my face, and when I had to go to the bank and sign the last paper, I said no thanks to their lawyer, I'll take care of my own windfall, wrote down my new account number, and had dinner out on the way home.

Well, I've already told you I don't have any family that I know of. I don't live in a small town up north. I don't want to encourage any of the political parties that I know of. And I am not a young woman with a hunger for new shoes or muscular men with their shirts off. What would you do? I will tell you what I did. You probably saw some of the events I staged.

I am not going to tell you exactly where I lived, but I can say that I had a regular-size condo not that far from the Pacific Ocean and within sight of some mountains that people ski on. Every once in a while I went to Toronto to see what life is like in the centre of the galaxy. While I was snooping around at some very small one-room art galleries, something I have always done, even before I could afford to buy pictures, I came across some small paintings, acrylic on plywood, I think, executed by someone named Aloys Niemann. You may have heard of him by now. At that time he was unknown and poorly dressed, and not for artistic reasons. I know this because I asked the curator of the show, a person who also appeared to have set up sleeping quarters in the gallery, whether I could meet the artist.

"You are interested in purchasing a painting?" he asked. And he waved a backhand toward the twelve pieces on his walls. There were no little red circles beside any of them.

"That is one of my objectives," I told him.

"He is a man of mystery," said the thirty-year-old curator, who had taken off his round eyeglasses and was now wiping their lenses with the tail of his plaid shirt.

"I think I can clear up this mystery," I said. "I have a hunch that I might be talking with him right now."

"If I were to tell you any more, I might be infringing on the artist-curator relationship," he said, putting his glasses back on, smeary as they still were, and smiling somewhat like a real estate agent.

"I am in possession of some funds that I wish to disburse in the direction of Canadian art," was my response.

"Call me Aloys," he said, his smile improving by the second.

I have to say that I found Aloys enjoyable in a number of ways, the majority of which I will not tell you about. Let's just say that I was particularly grateful for everything that resembled his skill with a paintbrush. I decided quite early on that I would like to commission him to do something creative and corrective at the same time, something I had always wished I could do.

I am not going to tell you the sum I bestowed upon him for his work, but I will tell you what the work entailed. You may remember the first performance piece. It happened at a little mall in Bloor West Village. Why did it happen? Because one day I was in a taxicab out there, and while the driver of the cab stopped to let a girl in a Rasta-coloured miniskirt jaywalk in front of us, I looked at a new fixture on the side of the street. It was a pair of fast-food eateries side by side in one building. Either side of the store had its own plastic logo sign. One said Wendy's. The other said Tim Hortons in a mock-cursive design.

"Let me out here," I said.

"But you told me you were going to Keele Street." Anyway, I think that's what he said.

"I have a terrible urge for a Dutchie," I said.

So I reconnoitered the site. Both the hamburger joint and the doughnut joint had red trademark signs on the outside wall of the building. In the case of the Tim Hortons, it was made of some kind of plastic in that stylized cursive signature. So here was what I wondered: was the crewcut hockey player from Timmins uncertain about whether his name had an "s" at the end, or did he always sign his name on his copies of Plato and Socrates to prove possession, and neglect to use an apostrophe for his purpose? Or did the cursive script on the advertising serve a purpose too arcane for my simple heiress's mind?

In any case I had seen my project, or rather Mr. Niemann's project. Frugally, I took a bus to the Kipling Station and rode the Bloor-Danforth subway most of the way home. I don't remember everything I thought about on that ride, of course, but I do remember wondering if the people who put the "s" at the end of "Horton" were saying something to the people who took the "e" off the end of Bloore when they named the street. And if you think that is important to my story, you are either right or indulgent.

Mainly I was thinking about Mr. Niemann's project. I paid him well for it, including the materials, and promised to take care of any legal expenditures. He impressed me with his intelligence, thoroughness and talent. What he did was:

– find out who made the Tim Hortons signs,

– go to that company and order an apostrophe in the right size,

– rent a truck and a ladder and coveralls with a name
  on back
– and put that apostrophe right up there between the
  "n" and the "s."

Then I made two telephone calls, and the next day there
were photographs of Aloys Niemann's newest installation
in the *Toronto Star* and the *Mississauga News*. I bought ten
copies of each paper. There had been some TV cameras at
the event too, but I had not summoned them. I don't know
much about TV.

Well, that was fun, but it was a pretty modest happening
or installation as far as happenings or installations go. Aloys
was game to proceed, and I was happy to find something to
spend my free money on. Call me the Canada Council Lite.

Our next art work took place in Perth County, at the home
of the Canadian Baseball Hall of Fame, located in a nice little town called, for some reason, St. Marys, whose nickname
is "The Stone Town." On one's approach from the Toronto
side there is a cute marker consisting of a kind of quarried
stone mantel with a curvilinear sign above it, along with an
image of a Victorian spire. ST. MARYS, it says just to the left
of the spire. This time I alerted the Stratford *Beacon Herald*
because St. Marys seemed to have just one of those newspapers that is not on paper, and I don't care for computer stuff
any more than I do for TV. I called the *Toronto Star* again, and
they sent a photographer, thank goodness, though he was
probably using one of those cameras with no film.

I thought that Aloys did a very nice job with the town's new apostrophe, though I was a little disappointed that a local crowd did not show up to protest the outside agitator vandalism. A couple of kids with bicycles stopped to watch. When Aloys got the lovely new punctuation in place, one of the kids shouted, "What the hell is that?"

We got back on the 401 highway without seeing any policemen, though I asked my chauffeur to take his time, and so we were a little disappointed. But we saw a picture on the first page of the provincial section of the *Star* the next day, along with a good little story speculating on the identity and next coup of the mysterious apostrophe artist. There was some expensive wine in Mr. Niemann's little apartment that night. I stayed a little later than I had intended to.

But among other things, there was planning to do. Performance art, even when it is of a guerrilla nature, involves preparation as much as it does performance. It would require more care and accuracy as the story grew. For a giddy moment we entertained the idea of changing "Maple Leafs" to "Maple Leaves" at the front door of the Air Canada Centre, but we decided against it because (1) it would be too difficult without a bigger crew, and (2) we were not sure that we had finished with apostrophes. It was not really a question of police interest or public damage; I had the funds to cover those eventualities.

Sometimes I found a sign that needed a possessive, and sometimes Aloys did. Sometimes he took it easy and spent the day correcting restaurant menus and greengrocer bins, sometimes adding apostrophes and sometimes crossing them out. The event at the famous Honest Eds store attracted a crowd of shoppers and more policemen than were required. Aloys had just finished providing a proper possessive on either sign at the corner of the building and was gathering his ladder and things when three cops moved in on him with the notion that they might want him to ride in their car. I don't know what they had planned for his equipment. I took care of the problem by walking across Bloor Street and throwing $50 bills to the breeze. Those three cops joined the rest of the constabulary in crowd control while I helped Aloys get his things in the van that was parked illegally in a lot on Palmerston.

Next day all four newspapers had photos of the sign and also the people in the crowd stooping like onion pickers. Two of the pictures featured accurate likenesses of my protege. I'm afraid we did a bit of giggling at the paint-daubed table in Aloys's kitchenette around noon.

Then we stopped giggling and sat looking into each other's watery eyes. Both of us had our glasses off. Other things, too.

"I guess I love you," he said.

I took a while to answer. While taking that while I reached for his painting hand and held it, as if for the first time. I felt serious all at once, and so I guess I sounded serious.

"Are you just saying that the way we say I just love Megan and her attitude?" I asked.

"No."

I held the back of his hand against my cheek as if I were a very young woman in a movie made for television.

"I don't know when it happened, but I just love you," he said, and he sounded pretty serious too, something he didn't much like doing.

"You are, I believe, thirty years old," I said.

"Thirty-one."

"While I am fifteen years older than you."

"Fourteen."

"I am your patron," I said.

He smiled a smile I had never seen on his whiskery face before.

"Do patrons always get as, um, close to their, um, what am I?"

"You are a promising artist."

He did not have a shirt on. There was not, I was so happy to have found out, a tattoo on his body. He had not shaped his torso and arms by going to a gym. He was thin, and though he was strong enough to climb ladders while carrying heavy things, he looked, oh, what is the right word? Elfin. That's not quite right, but I like the exaggeration of it.

He stood up now and stepped around the table. I can see clearly what he did and what I did next, but you can't.
In the next few weeks he did the sign hanging in front of the Kings Head pub, a bus shelter ad promoting "Drakes music," which we took not to be the quacking of a male duck, a number of those cute sayings that churches like to have on their lawn signs, and a billboard extravagantly touting a Celine Dion show at Caesars Palace. Well, at least we didn't have to deal with the usual bar-and-grill spelling: "Ceaser."

There were often people with cameras at our events now, and I don't remember how many times Aloys was asked for interviews. He wouldn't even give people his name. Once, at a bar called "Billy Joes" he was grabbed by a cop who had pushed his way through a crowd, but the manager told the cop that everything was copacetic. Said he had asked the artist to add the "comma thing." Good for business, he said, which was probably true. I had just given him a bit of mine.

As I think I have mentioned, Aloys often went off alone to save the life of the apostrophe, usually now trailing a posse made up partly of photographers and partly of people who just liked to be where photographers were. There were nights I spent alone at my hotel, which used to be my general practice, but which now made me a little antsy. I could have jumped into a limousine and gone to the airport and jumped onto a Boeing 777 and flown to Paris and jumped into a new outfit and had a drink and a cutlet at Silencio, but some teenage movie star drug addict would probably have been there.

Then one night I was alone in my rooms at the Ritz-Carlton and I got a funny feeling that worked on my brain the way okra works on your teeth. So when the telephone call came around six bells I suddenly felt encased in fate. Sure enough, it was the emergency ward at Brampton Civic Hospital, and thank heavens my name and phone number had showed up on a slip of paper in my lovely painter's thin wallet.

I did jump into a limousine, but asked the driver to go to Brampton instead of Malton. As we hurtled through the darkness I silently praised the traffic for being light and the driver for being quick. I know what I am doing, I said inside my head, I am trying to get to the person I love. At the hospital I tipped the cabbie $200 in fifties.

The only times I had seen a person so smashed up, covered in bandaging and connected to tubes and wires, was in movies and on television shows, and I don't mind saying that I felt yanked out of my place and time and body. They let me stay because of my appearance, I think. Here is where most writers will use the word "distraught," and rightly, because it means violently thrown out of your track, or something like that, I think.

"Maybe," they told me.

No matter the time it took to get there in the limo, I wasn't prepared for that.

"A chance," they said.

I wanted this to be happening to someone else, in some other place, maybe in a short story.

As often happens in such cases, I was told some time later, I felt guilty. I had commissioned him to use his talent and nerve to supply simple little elevated pieces of punctuation, and I had used some skill I have to make his performances newsworthy. I was carrying thousands of dollars but my artist was lying on his back in a hospital bed and totally unaware of the fact. I sat there for hours in a chair beside the windowless wall, listing all the things I could have inspired him to make.

It took a long time to get the story straight, and it probably is not totally straight yet. Some of it came out in the courtroom, in which I sat with my back straight and my eyes open. Aloys could not speak for a long time, even after the wires were taken out of his jaw, and when he could it was often impossible to understand what he was trying to say. The newspapers got it right about as much as they usually do. I managed to find a way to persuade one police officer to tell me as much as he could find out in all the paperwork. I had similar success with a bartender named Mario, who at first thought that there was a code encouraging bartenders to clam up in such cases. Multiple portraits of Robert Borden did the trick in either case.

So I can offer an account, a narrative that may employ the methodology of your average fiction, which, I suppose, really, is all you can ever expect when someone is telling you a story—of their life or anyone else's. And as you can tell, I am sort of reluctant to get to it. I will, though, as factually as can be expected.

Aloys was at a bar on Elliott Street near the Memorial Arena in Brampton, punctuating a menu on the wall. Apparently you could get "Shepards Pie" at that establishment. I don't know whether he was changing the spelling, but I think that we can be pretty sure that he was using his magic marker to supply the possessive. This activity aroused the curiosity of a thick man in a costume comprising motorcycle boots, tight blue jeans, a shaved head with tattoos up the neck, and a black leather vest.

I have not found out whether this establishment was a

motorcycle gang hangout, or whether Aloys learned that it was and went there to perform a new variation on his theme. Anyway, while the bald-headed thug was doing his best to read the altered menu, Aloys went around behind him and saw on the back of his black leather vest the image in profile of a humanoid skull with some kind of feathers streaming from its sides. Below the skull was a little square with the letters "mc" on it. Below all this, in red, and in caps, was the word "Ontario", and above all this were the words "Hells Angels", also in caps. Aloys still had his magic marker in his hand, so he put a correct apostrophe before the last letter of that second-to-last word.

Whether Aloys had consumed a beer or other alcohol in this bar or elsewhere, I have never found out, but whether he had or had not, you might expect that he would have noticed a number of these club members in the room. To put it briefly, a number of them, including the one now bearing acceptable punctuation, employed their fists and boots on Aloys for a long time. Drinkers who did not belong to their club went out the door. The bartender waited until the motorcyclists followed suit before he called 911, specifying ambulance.

In a lot of stories that might have been the climax. But I was not there, Aloys can't really tell me about it, and most of what I have read is constructed in the syntax favoured by policemen and lawyers. It's been a year since Brampton, and we are a long way from that place now. Let us say that I have found out what to do with all the money I inherited, and I am happy to say that I know what to do with my life. "Happy" is probably not the best word to use in this context, but I am just an amateur telling a tale I didn't choose, and if you happen to be an editor, you can go ahead and look for the right words.

I can tell you that Aloys looks at me with the eye that works, and he looks at me with a combination of love and apology. The apology is not his to give, I tell him. I apologize for getting him into this business in the first place. I am hoping that we get past apologies, and I hope that he is hoping so too. When I hold his right hand, he squeezes a little. I love that because he did not do it when we first came here.

By "here" I mean a lovely little bungalow with an addition I had built and specially equipped to rebuild a young artist with a lot of talent and a lot of potential and a lot of work ahead of him to reach at least toward the latter. In my research I had read a Hobart *Mercury* story that said that the Royal Hobart Hospital was going to cancel all elective surgery until the end of the financial year because of a $365 million shortfall in funding. You can guess what I did, though I have to tell you that a lot of people working for the governments involved were not easy to move. But now the people on that elective surgery wait list are happy, and the Royal Hobart nurses who spend part of their week up here in Austins Ferry are happy to be working with the latest in equipment ordered from my supplier in Glenorchy.

Yes, Austins Ferry. My computer's autocorrect has by now given up trying to insert a you-know-what. Austins Ferry is a northern suburb of beautiful Hobart, and arguably its chief claim to fame is a Catholic boys' school named St. Virgil's College. Go figure.

Ardell

Everyone told me she was bad news and that I had no business sniffing after her. My own mind said that I should never be within a kilometre of her, and that I should never say her name inside my skull. You know the way you do.

I don't even like the name Ardell. It has a kind of trailer trash edge to it. It's the kind of name your sister's shameful friend has. I tried to get her name out of my head by making up another name for her, a silly name: Saligia. Kind of salty, I figured.

I can't tell you when I first met her or even when I first saw her, not the way stories do. But back in the day, not all *that* long ago, when I used to go to a lot of parties at people's houses or in bars, she would be one of the people who were there.

For a long time we might cast our eyes, as they say, on each other, but we never had a conversation. We might say "hi" the way people do in order to get on to the next person,

but that was about it until the night of the Volkswagen Beetle. Well, I call it that because I can never remember even
what month it was, except that the streets were wet and I
was wearing my usual stupid jacket.

It started off there were six of us in the Volkswagen Beetle, getting rides home. That meant, you will know, that
there were four people in the back seat, and as usual I was
feeling the edge of panic, being under someone in the back
seat. Ardell was driving, it was her car, if I may be allowed to
continue this run-on sentence, and everyone was getting a
ride after an afternoon at that park on Twelfth where the Ja-
maicans play cricket. We all loved watching cricket, not
knowing the rules, enjoying the damp air, so it must have
been October, let's say.

As it turned out, I was the last of Ardell's passengers, and
there we were, coming back down Dunbar Street, when she
said more than one word to me for the first time.

"Let's go to the White Spot. You hungry?"

Okay, I think that you might want to skip the next paragraph. It has to do with what is coming, but I didn't write it.

The greedy glutton is the fiend's manciple. For he sticketh
ever in the cellar or in the kitchen. His heart is in the dishes;
his thought is all on the cloth; his life in the tun; his soul in
the crock. Cometh forth before his Lord besmutted and
besmeared, a dish in one hand, a bowl in the other. Babbleth
with words, and wiggleth as a drunken man that mindeth to
fall, beholds his great belly; and the fiend laugheth that he
bursteth.

If you did read that paragraph, I just have to add that

where you find "he" I found "she" doing just as well. But the image in that paragraph seems at first an illustration from an early printed volume and later a nineteenth-century cartoon.

Now that all the other human beings were out of the little car, I could see that it had been to the White Spot on other occasions. In fact it had been to various pizza places and hamburger joints, judging from the older and newer fast-food wrappers on the floor. There were other things all over the place, too, smallish items of clothing, squashed-open paperback novels, cigarette packages, plastic shopping bags and the like. I saw some loose change, too.

At the back of the White Spot there is a parking lot. A driver who doesn't want to go to the trouble of getting out of the car and into the building can just pull into a parking space, leave the headlights on, and wait for a server to take her order. The waiter provides a long tray that hooks onto the window slots on both sides of the front seat, and when the food arrives it is just under your chin.

Nowadays you can get just about any food known to the semi-foody world at the White Spot, but the restaurant was founded on hamburgers, back in the day before colourful fast-food joints appeared on every corner. Ardell ordered hamburger platters, which include French fries that have never been frozen, and coleslaw. She ordered three hamburger platters and two huge root beers.

"I don't know whether I can afford this," I said

"My treat," she said.

While we were waiting for our tray of food, Ardell smoked a cigarette. No thanks, I had said, and the windows were open. What could I say by way of objection? She attacked the cigarette. She was the noisiest cigarette smoker I had ever heard.

While we are waiting for the food to arrive, I should describe Ardell a little. Well, she was a lot.

Not fat. You wouldn't call her fat, or at least I wouldn't. She was what our grandparents used to call "pleasingly plump." Her clothes always seemed to be about to open, here and there. The top two buttons of her silk blouse, and another button halfway down, say. A zipper open a little. A sock slipped down and gathering at the top of her brown oxford. Ardell in her roundness threatening to come out through the spaces. When she lifted her weight to shift where she was sitting, she was bounty and peril at the same time.

She was slurping another cigarette when the uniformed young man arrived with our sustenance. I received my end of the long metal tray and hitched it into my window slot. By the time I had that done, she was halfway through her first hamburger. Paper napkins were falling to the floor. There was hamburger juice on her chin and then there was hamburger juice shining on the bare skin above her ample breasts. That is another word our parents would use— ample. On later occasions I would try to lick that juice off her, but this first time I just took furtive glances.

She was finishing the second hamburger, and was now pinching up French fries while I applied a little white plastic fork to my coleslaw. I went to pick up my half a hamburger but I was too slow. She let me share my fries with her and drained her root beer.

"Ready?" she asked. She had used her last paper napkin on her chin anyway. Then she had dropped it somewhere.

I proffered the rest of my root beer in its big heavy glass mug. She shook her head and turned on the headlights to signal the guy to come and retrieve the tray. I dropped a dollar and something on it. Remember, this was in the day when you could drink beer all night for two bucks.

To tell the truth, I was both put off and turned on by this scene. The inside of a Volkswagen Beetle is not what you would call commodious, and Ardell was filling more than her share of it, so I think I can be excused for feeling a kind of underfed desire, if you want to use that kind of language.

Later on I would sometimes wonder whether I were listing her seven items or my own. Of course there were more than seven, but the others were all redundant or venal at most.

Anyway, I think that you will agree that a slightly overweight woman while she is still pretty young is more attractive, let's say desirable, than a slightly skinny one. I agree with my friend Will that what he calls "kachunga" kegs are a turn-on, while those legs you see models strutting down the runway on are off-putting. Oh, there are probably some strange guys who like those emaciated ones, I don't know.

I thought she was going to invite me in at her place, but instead she dropped me off at my place. I was and am pretty slow when it comes to sparking a girl, but I did manage to suggest that we might see one another again, not in a crowd at a smoke-filled house but as two people, or maybe half of four people.

"Can you cook?" she asked.

"I am more of a warm-things-up person," I said.

"Maybe I can teach you."

"To cook."

"Don't get smart, Delsing," she said. "Not right yet."

As she Volkswagened away I wondered what those last three words were meant to convey. Then I thought oh hell, if anything is going to happen, it will happen. I had books to read, essays to write, a laundromat to visit.

One of the books I had to read and write an essay about was Dante's *Inferno*. I found two things interesting about Dante's visit to the nether reaches. One, he met a lot of people he had known above-ground in Italy. And two, he noticed that the punishments down there were always creatively fitted to the bad things the sufferers had done up in Florence or wherever. So the guy that hoarded belongings all his life has to walk around with all his furniture tied in a pile on his back. The guy that cheered for the New York Yankees gets hit over the head all day with a Louisville Slugger.

I made that one up.

But here is what the lazy gink has to face in eternity. He has to spend almost every minute of every day, running as fast as he can. In fact, most of the people in hell don't even have minutes and days, but only a kind of fiery eternity. The lazy gink? The sloth? Constant running, and constant checking of wristwatch.

Well, back to the present, or rather what the present was back then, and I am hoping that you are not tired of smart cracks about time, but I'll understand if you are. I had just got inside the door to the basement in which I had a room at the time, when I heard the screech of Volkswagen brakes and a toot of Volkswagen horn.

Out I went and there she was. I didn't ask myself where she got the chocolate bar but she was holding it in one hand and the steering wheel in the other. She didn't have to say, "Get in." At this moment, a lot of people would have offered their passenger a bite.

I don't have to describe getting there and getting inside the building and inside her basement suite. A basement suite in those days meant more than one room. More than one room meant a kitchen and a room with a bed and a desk in it. In another corner of the basement there was a toilet and shower and sink in a little cubby.

It's how we lived in those days, and we never imagined what we would live like now, or at least I didn't.

There was a little table in the kitchen, and two chairs. I seized the moment by brushing food wrappers off one of the chairs and sitting on it. I did not take off my coat because I had taken it off at my place. There were items of clothing hanging from most things.

"Baby ants," I said. "Strawberry seeds, my bank account, the chance that the Red Sox will win the American League pennant."

"What are you on about?" she asked, from up close.

"That's small talk," I said, and if I had been holding a book open I would have snapped it shut. I prized my wit, especially in moments when I was nervous.

"I guess I have to find a way to put an end to that," she said, and she leaned down and kissed me on the forehead, then on the mouth. I could taste chocolate and peanuts.

Along with her size came a little more than average strength. It is to that strength that I attribute the fact that I was quickly into the other room, propelled by hands that were insistent and perhaps still holding food. Down on the bed I went and down on me she went, in all ways of understanding that phrase. Her clothing seemed to come off without help as she applied her eager attention to mine.

You are not going to get a detailed sex scene here, but I would like to mention a few things. It was pretty loud. It went on for a long time. Just about every fluid you can imagine showed up here and there. Many times I lay flat, trying to catch my breath, happy to have survived—just before she seized me for more.

I would have to say that before that night and early morning I had experienced less poontang than the average young man. I figure that Ardell had me caught up by mid-morning. I know that there was not one part of my body that she had not had in her mouth and vice, as they say, versa.

It was not that I didn't have somewhere to go in the late morning; it is just that I didn't go there. I stayed, exhausted, in Ardell's messy bed. Once I saw her reach toward her cigarette package and give up when it looked as if she would have to get out of bed to get a smoke.

"You want a cup of coffee?" she asked, about eleven.

"Matter of fact I would," I said.

But she was not about to get up and make me one.

I was getting itchy to go, but too damned tired. If Ardell was itchy anywhere she was just a bit too lazy to scratch. I did wonder how she could go so long without a pizza or a sandwich.

And so we dozed the day away, except for those times when Ardell had to have a little more of me.

I think I remember getting to classes the next day, and I know I do remember that during the weeks that followed, I got to see Ardell eat a lot more junk food and impulse purchases from the supermarket. Once I watched without saying a word, while she went through two long packages of fig squares. If I had been a refrigerator she would have gone through me in a single night. Okay, that is an exaggeration, but I do remember her consuming me greedily on many a night, on many a carpet or porch or staircase.

I say "greedily" with justification.

Have you ever seen one of those big shiny stuffed toads with stitches down the belly and maybe the word "Nicaragua" across the back? They shine as if shellacked and are usually as big as you would ever want a toad to be. They are the sort of thing one might bring back from a trip to Central America, as one might bring baby alligator-claw earrings from Louisiana. I brought one back from Costa Rica because I couldn't afford an expensive souvenir. It disappeared the last time I got married.

Well, Ardell had them all over her place. They were all colours of the toad community, and all of them pretty big.

They were on flat surfaces all over her place, including the floors. They had names from Mexico to the Philippines. Some were on top of others. I think that Ardell thought of herself as a collector. Maybe I should have too. Can you call someone a toad hoarder?

One night I finally asked her, "What's with all the frogs?"

"Toads," she said. "I am not a frog girl."

"Why so many? Wouldn't one toad do? Maybe two?"

What a stupid bit of dialogue, I was thinking. I think I was avoiding a discussion of something else, some other behaviour.

"If I could do it, I would have them all, all the stuffed toads in the world."

"You are an appetite girl," I said.

"Give me that," she said, and she did not reach for a toad.

A lot of people think that being greedy is a way of showing your egotism, but I don't think that was the way with Ardell. Have you ever known a boy who wants to eat all the time, who's just hungry? I think it was that way with Ardell about everything, the hamburgers, the stuffed toads, me, the highway lane with no traffic in it. She drove her Beetle hungrily, and while she did so, buttons slid out of their buttonholes in her blouse.

She satisfied her appetite whenever she could. While she was finishing a third bagel with cream cheese, I might sarcastically suggest thinking about the starving children in some sub-Saharan forest.

"Africa!" she said, while I reached across the table and took the dab of cream cheese from her lovely chin and poked my finger in her mouth. "Lots of people I know have been to Africa! I never get to go to Africa! I will never see the Zamboni River!"

"Zambezi."

"Or that one. Why the hell should Margot Thiesman get to sail up the Zamboni, while I have to sit here starving in an overlit joint named after a dead football player?"

"Ice hockey."

I knew that she was kidding. She did have virtues, and while none of them were on any Church list that I know about, they made me want to be with her. One of them was her sense of humour, especially her sense of humour about herself.

"Look at that woman in that huge BMW," she said once, while making a lane change that caused lots of sound nearby. "Why does that little snip get that big roomy sedan while I have to operate a vehicle I am wearing as much as driving?"

"Maybe if you shovelled out some of the food wrappers and old psychology magazines, there would be more room," I suggested, hoping that we were in comic mode.

"Hold the wheel," she said, while tearing the plastic off a pepperoni stick.

"Thou shalt not covet thy neighbour's automobile," I continued.

Maybe people who are hungry all the time are bound to be envious. I had a picture flash through the part of my mind that was not occupied by fright related to our path among fast cars. There was smooth, curvy Ardell standing on the side of a pond, but her head was a dog's head, and in the dog's mouth was a bone.

Now I know that if the picture had not been replaced by my quick concern for the pedestrian who was considering the promised safety of the crosswalk, I would have seen Ardell the canine looking down at her reflection in the pond and dropping her bone as she tried to get the reflected one that was just now rising from the other dog's mouth.

Everyone told me they weren't jealous of me for having a fling or relationship with Ardell. By jealous you mean envious, I said. Whatever, they said. It's your funeral. That's just a figure of speech, isn't it, the part about a funeral, I said. I said it to myself again later. I whispered, "Hedda," just to tempt the little fates in the shadows around me.

You can skip that paragraph, too. Actually, it's too late for that, isn't it?

All right, you are going to say, here was a young woman who was not skinny the way modern advertising said she was supposed to be, who ate eagerly and greasily, like a Labrador retriever at a bowl of Alpo, who left a trail of detritus that she couldn't bother picking up, who shamelessly devoured her partner in bed and on the floor, who had to have more than her share of everything, and who begrudged anyone else who had what she wanted, from the last slice of pizza to the passing lane on Highway 1. Here's the question: why are you still within a city block of her?

Here is the question you might have asked if you'd had the luck to be in my position: who does she think she is?

I never had the nerve to ask her that, or maybe I just thought it wasn't my place to ask her. If she would lift her face from what she was doing to me and say, "You are one lucky son of a bitch, Delsing," who was I to contradict her? So I understood, when she took the passing lane from someone who might have had it first, she may as well have shouted that the other driver was privileged to be on the same freeway. If Solomon had been riding with us, he might have said, you know the Lord hates seven things, and the first one I have to mention is a proud look. What's his name when he's at home, she probably would have answered, reaching across me to get the Big Turk out of the glove compartment.

"I went to Sunday School as much as you did, Delsing," she said to me one time while I was trying to catch my breath. "I still read the Bible. Do you?"

"Once in a while," I said.

"I was reading that dork Paul's letter to the Galatians last week. I know all there is to know about his wages of the flesh. You got anything against my flesh?"

"Often," I said.

"There you go," she said. "You are right now as close to heaven as you are ever going to get."

"Wasn't heaven I was worried about," I said, kind of quietly.

"What?"

"Nothing. Nothing. Speaking of being close to heaven, how do you feel about tall buildings?"

"I am not afraid of heights, if that's what you mean."

"You know we are in a serious earthquake zone?"

"Show me a tower," she said, nabbing a parking spot someone else had been waiting for, "and I'll go to the top."

Now would probably be a good time to tell you how it ended, our relationship, I guess you'd call it.

I had, of course, heard what she had to say when another driver wounded her sense of proper automotive behaviour. I had heard how loudly she could exclaim when the dough-nut she had just consumed had been the last one in the box. But these reactions, I took it, were meant to be largely humorous. I did once see her throw a toaster across her kitchen after it had malfunctioned, the sort of thing that small appliances often did to their owners. Once, when I filled in a few squares in her Friday morning *New York Times* crossword, she crumpled the newspaper in her two hands and began eating it. I managed to laugh a bit while I pulled a few headlines out of her mouth.

But one night when, I have to admit, we were both bathed, as they say, in perspiration, I reached into the drawer of the bedside table and retrieved the only chocolate bar there, a Crispy Crunch, as I recall. She stared at me in a way that was supposed to draw my hand toward her. But I raised the bar, unwrapped it, and placed crispy in my mouth. A second later crunch followed.

These actions were quite unlike me, as you have likely gathered.

I had retrieved chocolate bars from that drawer on earlier occasions, but on those occasions, the chocolate bars were employed to join a few of Ardell's appetites. That is to say, they had been allowed to melt between our heated bodies and then provide a snack both sweet and salty.

Not this time.

It started with a roar you might expect from a sea lion that had been exposed to a Cher Christmas music CD. My skin crawled, then tried to snap back. I jumped naked out of bed and stood for only a second or two before the missiles started to hit me and miss me. The soft ones came first—bedclothes and pillows. Then a clock, an ashtray, a small chair. All this while the roar was turning into a wail such as an animal in a bad dream might make, an animal you think you might have heard of in childhood. I tried to find my clothes, and then I gave that plan up and tried to get out of the room. Things kept hitting me. I knew that when she ran out of things I would become a thing, and I knew that she would not be satisfied to throw me once. Bolts of lightning were coming out of her nostrils. An oil fire crept up the front of her torso. I had to get away from the sound that was trying to join my eardrums together. I made it out of the room just before napalm bloomed across the floor.

I pulled a curtain off the little living room windows and made it to the street only half naked. Flames were leaping from every window on the block, and I could hear sirens approaching. I walked in my bare feet on disgusting sidewalks all the way home, arriving in the darkness without a

key. I used the curtain to make my fist quiet as it broke a
basement window.

I understood that such a scene is something you were not
supposed to keep bottled up, but I was in no mood to hear
people say that they had warned me, you see? I finally did
tell my friend Dorothy because before she went to work at
the Bank of Commerce, she took a major in psychology at
U.B.C. Dorothy told me that Ardell was angry at herself. It
wasn't me she wanted to kill. That made me feel a lot better, as you might imagine.

2. In Fairness

I had seen him giving me the eye at four or five parties. He
thought he was being casual, but men that age tend to over-
rate their subtlety. After a few times I started coming to
house parties and bars with a fair amount of cleavage showing. It wasn't that I was looking for someone to bop—I
guess I just felt like giving some young Lothario a lesson. Of
course it turned out that he wasn't a young Lothario. He
was just young.

One night after a party had run out of beer and wine I gave
a bunch of people rides home. I don't remember whether I
offered him a lift or whether he climbed into the back of my
VW along with several other people. Whatever, he was sitting in the front seat after everyone else had been dropped

off. I have no idea what he was expecting. He was a kind of a smartass, you know, the kind of guy that isn't very sure of himself and has to chatter inanities, hoping that that will make things occur that will just happen to him. I usually find a way to piss these guys off. I decided to give this one a chance. I took him to the drive-in burger place.

What was going on here? Partly I wanted to initiate him, and partly I was hungry after a night of beer and wine and cigarettes and no nooky, you should pardon my vocabulary.

Not that I was thinking of the last-named activity with this guy. What kind of future was there with a guy whose name is a present participle? He was skinny but not lithe, if you get what I mean. He always wore white shirts, and they were always a little unevenly tucked in. His hair was limp and tended to fall in his face, and he could have used some clippers up his neck. His shoes looked as if somebody in the military had thrown them away, and there were two pens in his shirt pocket. I had heard rumours that he thought of himself as a young poet, but he looked more like an extra in a dirty movie set in a motel.

I guess he had a pretty good voice, and I suppose I was interested to see whether there was a scrap-end of something potentially redemptive down inside somewhere. When the carhop arrived in his uniform made of unnatural materials, I ordered quite a few hamburgers and very large milkshakes. When the stuff came, I saw that it took him forever just to execute the simple act of unwrapping a burger. I was started on my second before he selected a French fry. When he wasn't looking I undid another button on my shirt.

I wanted to wipe the second half of my second burger on his face.

"Are you going to church later this morning?" I asked him.

"I am spiritual but not religious," is what he said.

"I wish I had a cheeseburger for every time I have heard that boast," I told him.

He sulked a while, and bit about a millimetre off his burger.

"You are fastidious," I said. "You are guilty of temperance. You should have been a climate," I added, hoping he might figure it out.

When I lit up a cigarette as one would do after a snack in those days, he rolled his window back down. He didn't object to my cig, and he did not get all high and mighty about being an abstainer. There was just a certain *feel* in the air, and damn it, I decided to push things. I let my shirt come loose on his side. After the carhop had left with the long tray, our hero was left with a balled-up napkin in his right hand. He was looking for a place to deposit it, as if all Volks drivers had sanitary disposal units in their coupés. I took the almost unmarked tissue away from him and tossed it on top of the other stuff already on the floor behind us. Then I sighed deeply and made as much noise as I could sucking on my cigarette.

When I dropped him off at his grotto, he didn't suggest anything salubrious, so I drove home feeling a mixture of itchiness and pissedoffedness. Or most of the way home. For some reason the image I had of this loser in his poorly-chosen garments was replaced by an image of him without them, an awkwardly stick-legged demi-virgin weighing about as much as an average German shepherd. Dog, that is. It's not that I was partial to muscleless undergrads with bad haircuts. I guess I was just angry enough and horny enough to subject this poor shnook to a sleepless night.

I honked my horn outside his basement window and told myself one candy bar and I'm off. I was just started on the second one when he came out the door, a well-tucked white shirt in the surrounding gloom. It was a cool November evening, and this spider didn't even have his own web. I took him home and asked him the four questions I would allow him before taking him apart.

"Are you a little afraid?"

"Not exactly afraid," he said, and he carried a plate and a fork over to my sink. "A little nervous, maybe."

"Are you excited?"

"More like confused," he said, while sweeping crumbs off the table onto his other hand. "Is this an examination?"

"Are you hungry? Thirsty?"

"Nope. It's pretty near the end of the day. I think I've pretty well consumed all I really need for one day." He actually turned my gas station calendar to November. Picture of a mechanic with no shirt on.

"Do you mind if I eat something?"

I think he caught the look in my eyes at last.

"Uh, uh . . ." was all he could say before I lowered a shoulder and propelled him into the other room. There were a few books on the bed, but I took him for a reader anyway. He was intent on removing his glasses and getting them safely on my bedside table. He had to push some stuff off it first.

I pretty well had to show him everything. He might have been a thirteen-year-old boy, he was so slow. He growled some but he wouldn't say a word. I gobbled him and then I said words that opened his eyes wide. I think I shook the rest of his words out of him, he was so quiet. Quietly, he held a handful of me in his hand and in his other hand. He was mainly bones himself, and I think that he was gaga over a quantity of what he would later call pulchritude. I get this all the time from semi-educated Lotharios. They think pulchritudinous means amply desirable. Well, it originally meant speckled, like a perch.

For the rest of that night and well into the next day I was his fish. It was not that I couldn't get enough of him. It was just that there was not all that much to get. And it was not until early afternoon that he was too exhausted to try tidying up after each episode.

I showed Mr. Fastidious a lot of new things over the next few weeks. I surprised him, as they used to say, on my balcony, in my car parked on a downtown street, in the scant woods on the edge of the university campus. I could not persuade him to come into the Safeway washroom with me. And I could not make him skip any classes.

"I'll do more than Milton can to justify his way to man," I promised him.

"It's God's ways," he said, quick as a wink. "And you aren't malt."

"I am champagne, and you are too sober by far," I informed him.

"But I am not your toad," he said, referring to my fine collection of inert amphibians.

"You had better check your belly for stitches every morning when you wake up," I suggested.

"You are a slave to your appetites," he said, edging away. But not quickly enough. I grabbed what there was left of him.

And so it went. I think that I introduced him, among other things, to his first really thorough conflict regarding his own self-image. He really really wanted to be good. He told me in one of his many moments of weakness that he had made a deal with God or someone like that to be a true straight arrow. He would never smoke, never drink spirits, never stray from the virginal path and then the faithful path, never use idle curse words, and who knew what else. This was a kid, I imagined, who wished that Moses had come down off that mountain with *three* tablets. I think he would have been proud of his life plans if pride weren't a sin.

In other words, here I was for the first time in my life, up against, as they say, mister chastity, temperance, charity, diligence, patience, kindness and humility. He would have been the rebel devil who sailed up out of Hell right into the parking garage in Heaven.

But on the other hand (and foot, and other parts that were not extremities) he squirmed when he could have squirmed away from an eyelash under a scrotum. I taught him to say "yes please" and "right there, yes there," at the correct time. If he was not experiencing a conflict, he was practicing the divine or diabolic art of being two different people in the same bed, which, I might add, has always been just fine with me.

One night or early morn, while gently puffing on a cigarette and enjoying the weight of his sleeping head on my far shoulder, I came to wonder. Is it that I have freed his second self to share this bed, or is it maybe that we are one self, together at last? I would be a very happy *yin* to his *yang*. I had encountered my share of yangs, and Delsing's was if anything average, but I have to admit that I had taken my own behaviour more for granted before coming up against the seven deadly virtues.

That idea got me thinking about these numbers. All right, I thought, let us admit that seven is a good number for deadly sins. Seven is nice. One for each day of the week. Seven is a prime number, and all that magic stuff. But why did we have to have the seven big-deal virtues to go up against them? Why didn't God or Pope Gregory come up with, say, eighty-five holy virtues, outnumber those sins and send them scurrying home with their yangs between their legs?

Then Delsing could have made an honest woman out of me.

Sure.

But here is the thought I came to about the same time that the sleeping saint last put his unconscious hand on my lower belly. I was created to test his resolve, to see whether he could rely on his childhood oath to keep him away from temptation. Or better, to experience temptation and call up his reserves of won't power to. No, that kind of thought is for those who go to church and are afraid to let themselves walk into the deep middle of religion. Submerge. Or the opposite—make up a story in which the lusted one goes berserk and has to be escaped with one's still-quite-virtuous life. For years from then on, he could lie in bed alone, with a fond smile on his face. What I am saying is that maybe I was an angel sent to make a complete human being out of the boy with the trembling mouth.

• • •

ABOUT THE AUTHOR

George Bowering is a distinguished novelist, poet, editor, professor, historian and tireless supporter of fellow writers, Bowering has authored more than one hundred books and chapbooks, including works of poetry, fiction, autobiography, biography and fiction for young readers. His writing has been translated into French, Spanish, Italian, German, Chinese and Romanian. His novel, Burning Water, won the Governor General's award for fiction and his memoir, Pinboy, was short-listed for the B.C. National Award for non-fiction in 2013. In 2002, Bowering was recognized by the Vancouver Sun as one of the most influential people in British Columbia. In 2011 he was awarded the Lieutenant Governor's Award for Literary Excellence.